Jonathan Seidler is an auth

His work has been published frequently in *The Guardian*, *The Sydney Morning Herald*, *The Australian* and *GQ*. Jonathan launched two nationally syndicated fiction series for *Broadsheet* and commissioned, edited and published an anthology of nature writing. He also wrote and performed the score for *Snare*, officially selected for SXSW and Tribeca, and most recently was music supervisor on the SBS series *Latecomers*. Jonathan's first book, *It's A Shame About Ray*, was adapted for an immersive live performance for Sydney Writers' Festival. He is an *Esquire* columnist, where he writes weekly about the culture of men, mental health and fatherhood.

*This book is soundtracked by many musical references.*
*Scan this code to listen to its official playlist as you read.*

JONATHAN SEIDLER

# ALL THE BEAUTIFUL THINGS YOU LOVE

MACMILLAN
Pan Macmillan Australia

Pan Macmillan acknowledges the Traditional Custodians of Country throughout Australia and their connections to lands, waters and communities. We pay our respect to Elders past and present and extend that respect to all Aboriginal and Torres Strait Islander peoples today. We honour more than sixty thousand years of storytelling, art and culture.



First published 2024 in Macmillan by Pan Macmillan Australia Pty Ltd
1 Market Street, Sydney, New South Wales, Australia, 2000



NATIONAL LIBRARY OF AUSTRALIA

A catalogue record for this book is available from the National Library of Australia

Typeset in 12.2/17pt Adobe Garamond Pro by Midland Typesetters, Australia

Printed by IVE

The quotation on page vii is from *Essays in Love* by Alain de Botton, Picador, 1993.

The author and the publisher have made every effort to contact copyright holders for material used in this book. Any person or organisation that may have been overlooked should contact the publisher.

FSC www.fsc.org MIX Paper from responsible sources FSC® C018183

The paper in this book is FSC® certified. FSC® promotes environmentally responsible, socially beneficial and economically viable management of the world's forests.

*To Keren,*

*Much like life, without you, this book would have been terrifically boring.*

*Ti amo.*

*One of love's greatest drawbacks is that, for a while at least, it is in danger of making us seriously happy.*

*– Alain de Botton*

# ALL THE BEAUTIFUL THINGS YOU LOVE

# THE END, WHERE IT BEGINS.

ELLY AND ENZO break up the same way we all do. Like gum in the sole of a Reebok trainer, they stubbornly refuse to extricate themselves from a union rapidly going rank in the height of English summer. When we encounter the couple for the first time, they have been together for ten years and married ten months. Elly, who is not a screamer, is screaming. Enzo, who rarely cries, is tearing up. There is a forgotten curry on the hob and during this détente, it simmers, curdles, then burns, sending acrid wafts of smoke through the flat and eventually setting off the fire alarm.

As their neighbours alert the authorities, Enzo is shoving clothes into the oversized tote bag he and Elly usually use to do the shopping. Academy Apartments, where they have lived for most of their relationship, is a converted school; all the flats are open-plan reinterpretations of science labs and history classrooms with very few partitions. There is nowhere to go, and so Enzo is unable to escape, enveloped by spice and smoke and shouting and an uncomfortable thump in his lower abdomen that indicates this is almost definitely a Serious Life Crossroads Moment. He should walk back into the kitchen like a sensible person, embrace his new wife and try earnestly to salvage the past decade of his life. But far from being sensible, Enzo is better known for always having a great tale to tell over a few pints, which goes a long way towards explaining why he jumps out the precariously placed ground-floor window and scurries past the inbound firemen instead.

Enzo is in his early thirties, typically adorned in the inoffensive stubble and pale blue Uniqlo Oxford shirt that counts as a uniform for his generation. He has remarkable eyes and an unremarkable career writing paid financial services content that he still tells his parents back in Italy is 'journalism'.

Elly, a few years older than Enzo, has made bangs her trademark since before they came back for the third time. She is taller than you are imagining, owns too many Ottolenghi cookbooks – she likes the way the spines look arranged on her shelf – and has undiagnosed endometriosis.

Enzo will tell you he met Elly by pure chance, at a friend's do where he'd arrived late, already high off a few balloons and on the way to a sweaty Klaxons gig in Brixton, in the winter of 2007.

Elly knows that Enzo actually saw her across the room at The Shacklewell Arms a few weeks prior, which was not difficult to imagine as we have already ascertained she is quite tall.

He badgered many of her friends at the bar until he found out her name.

Enzo says he was obsessed from the very first minute.

Elly does not dispute this fact.

Nobody goes looking for their life partner at twenty-three, says Enzo. But sometimes it's taken out of your hands.

She anoints him Darling first, but she fucking loves it when he calls her Babe.

Enzo realises within five minutes of shouty conversation at the aforementioned party that Elly is not only funnier than he is, but also significantly more intelligent.

The first thing Elly notices is that Enzo doesn't remark upon her height. He just stands on his tiptoes to kiss her like it's something he's always known how to do.

Neither of them will admit it, but they both still have a soft spot for the Klaxons.

Academy Apartments sits at the lip of a five-point intersection so notoriously difficult to cross in a straight line that they even named a lager in its honour. A sprawling, labyrinthine oasis, the building touches multiple roads while somehow absorbing none of their noise. It's an incomprehensibly large property, flanked by an overground and underground station and with three separate bus stops along its perimeter. Within its vast walls lives an impossibly unquantifiable number of tenants, landlords, long-term lessees, short-stay Airbnbs, hangovers from last week's illegal rooftop rave still too high to brave the stairs and the odd Hackney stray that's managed to tailgate through the second of four security doors and is now at a loss as to how to get back out again. Few have lived in the complex long enough to remember the school that has since been subsumed, but it surely must have been massive if the number of dwellings is anything to go by. The last time there were students at Academy Apartments, Supergrass had only just been caught by the fuzz.

Elly and Enzo rent a flat on the ground level, with mosaic floors, swinging double doors and noticeboards clearly left over from the building's previous life. With its stupendously high ceilings and magnificent arched windows that stream in light in the afternoons, it's almost too much space for East London, where £2000 pcm is more likely to get you a cupboard and a non-functioning toilet to fight over with four other flatmates.

A cat called Lola, or Lulu, or Layla, traipses the cold and endless hallways of the Academy. She is a beautiful ginger tabby with faultless fur, far too pristinely turned out to be a stray. One afternoon in late March, not long after they finally affix all their artwork to the exposed brick walls, she appears outside Enzo and Elly's flat, mewling by the front entrance, before padding her way over to the sofa like she's always been there, which perhaps she has. Everyone in their wing of the building has a different theory about who Lola belongs to. Oli next door is convinced it's the cool couple in 74 who always seem to have the kind of dinner parties you only see in films. John across the hall insists it's Jude in No. 12, an elder guardian of the Academy, who was a secret songwriter in the '80s and sort of looks like Joni Mitchell if you ever manage to glimpse her face through the out-of-control house plants and stacks of vintage teacups. The important thing is that nobody is right, which means everyone can reasonably claim ownership, including Elly and Enzo, delighted at the frequent return of their adorable house guest, who proves a fitting distraction for their own issues.

Enzo and Elly get together during the unusually warm spring of 2007; nights of long strolls and shared cigarettes, open-air BBQs wafting through London Fields, cut fruit from M&S, sticky sex and cider Sundays. It's a slow, sensuous type of season that the people who write the sort of books Elly and Enzo devour one after another love to rhapsodise over. Days seem to last weeks. Enzo, with his Mediterranean blood, luxuriates in the heat, skin turning mocha as he dials out of work and into his annual pursuit of hedonism. For Elly, it is an ideal time to enter a relationship, already safe in the knowledge that this is as good as it gets, that everything beyond this high watermark will simply be trying to recapture what is already gone.

It is the spring when a Scottish producer calling himself Calvin Harris is unleashed on house parties for the first time, before the Vegas residences and shirtless Armani billboards. It is the spring when David Beckham returns to England after a year abroad, to draw with Brazil at a newly reopened Wembley. It is also the spring before the wettest UK summer ever recorded, when thousands of Britons are rescued from floodwaters as Enzo struggles to hold a flimsy pound-shop umbrella effectively over his new girlfriend while they walk back to the Tube station after dinner.

Enzo and Elly fall apart during the heatwave of 2018, best remembered for riots outside local lidos, the mass shoplifting of ice lollies by frustrated youths unable to escape to the sea breeze of Ayia Napa, the tracks of the Overground melting under pressure from the relentless sun, raging bushfires in Manchester and an entire nation of English fans dedicating Atomic Kitten's '[Football's Coming] Home Again' to Gareth Southgate, only to discover on perhaps the most unbearably hot night of the year, at about the same moment as Elly's curry is bubbling over and threatening to test the lifetime guarantee on her favourite Le Creuset, that football isn't coming home again after all.

Red-eyed and shell-shocked, Enzo does not appear at all out of place as he stumbles down Mare Street in search of an Extremely Strong Drink. The pubs are teeming with Lions fans in mourning, too wankered to go home or remember how to dial their dealers, escaping the sauna of their neighbourhood boozer, sucking in offensively warm air and trying valiantly not to cry. Enzo, who despite his origins has never given a toss about football, is not beyond the poetry of the moment, this stinking summer evening when the sun hasn't even begun setting over Regent's Canal and already countless lives – just like his – have been completely ruined.

It's tempting to follow Enzo, undoing one too many buttons on his already sweat-slicked shirt as he elbows his way through the red and white grievers, across a floor littered with broken pint glass towards the commencement of his much-needed oblivion. But convention and curiosity dictate that richer tales often arise from those who are left behind, so we pan back across the streets of stragglers looking for exuberant Croatian fans to start a fight with, hooking left at Hackney Central on the way to that infernal intersection, where crushed cans gleam on the sidewalk, and finally through the security doors to Elly who, having finally dispatched the friendly firefighters, sits cross-legged on her purple couch with Lola the cat in her lap and starts mentally compiling a list of all the stuff she needs to sell.

# I. BICYCLE

THE SKY IN London high summer is a pinnacle of graphic design. A steadfast blue with no fixed centre, bleeding orange and yellow at the fringes, dye that runs off into a false horizon, hovering among the pubs and council flats. In the park, where Elly cycles laps to forget about Enzo, the atmosphere swoops dangerously close to the desiccated grass, every turn a brilliant lens flare. London summer evenings don't fade so much as melt, and as she rounds the far double gates of Vicky Park, where the lake is now darker than the sky it reflects, Elly enthusiastically soaks it in.

When Enzo bought her the bike for her birthday, already adjusted for her height and wrapped in chrome silver, the only colour he correctly assumed would complement her monochromatic wardrobe, he insisted she learn to ride without hands. Elly, having not been on two wheels since a disastrous series of spills on Regent's Canal during her first year as a Londoner led her to believe she was simply too gangly to manoeuvre any type of vehicle, was instantly dubious.

'No hands? What are you, twelve?'

'Don't be funny. It's amazing. There's no feeling like it.'

'What if I wobble?' she asked. 'I could fall.'

'No.' He looked directly in her eyes with the earnestness that made him attractive to almost all women and a fair number of men. 'It is all, how do you say, mental.'

'Are you saying I'm mental?'

'Yes,' he said, clasping her hands excitedly and completely missing the gag. 'There is nobody more mental than you.'

It doesn't take Elly nearly as long as expected to get back on the saddle, using the pumping power of her legs to steady the frame of the machine as she tentatively practises removing one hand, ever so slightly, from the brown faux leather handlebars, and then soon enough, the second. With practically zero fanfare, she becomes a devil on two wheels as she and her boyfriend glide through the park at sunset, pedalling swiftly down straight paths before leaning back and hitting cruise control.

Enzo grew up whipping around the back streets of Naples on scooters with his two sisters yelling at him to go faster, and had long ago abandoned any lingering sense of physical danger. He was right; the sensation of propelling forward on a bicycle without holding it was truly singular, so freeing it almost felt like flying at a low altitude. Elly soon found that she could achieve higher speeds when she wasn't crouched over, her bike frame capturing vignettes of the turquoise-Tuscan ombré that spilled across her field of vision as she sat back, arms by her sides, in a deep flow state.

Once, on a particularly long stretch between the pub and the park's edge, Enzo had reached out for her hand while they were in motion. It hadn't lasted long, but the tandem connection had the crackle of something timeless and graceful, like a scene from a silent movie. As they came apart just before Royal Gate West, both realised something wonderful had just occurred. They had sex three times that same night, inexplicably hungry for one another and buoyed by their seeming transgression of basic physics.

Now she rides these same routes as a single woman. Her bike, Roxy, still shimmers, but it's more of a dull gleam. She is considering – always considering – getting rid of it. As she hits a straight patch, her muscle memory kicks in and she digs deep, long legs charging like pistons against the pedals. Within fifty yards, she's going so fast the trees are melding with the sky like a bad watercolour. Her hands come off the bars and rise to her face. It is a strange place for an emotional outburst, but then Elly is quite a strange person. She sobs as she speeds through the evening, hoping that a large stick or sudden distraction will wipe her out, replacing the lacerating pain in her soul with something more tangible.

'Wow. That was mad!'

'I told you.'

'It was like I was flying.'

'I'm so glad you liked it,' he said, holding her by the waist. 'My mama, she always tell me it's these little things we remember.'

It is loop after flawless loop. Elly will never wobble, she knows these interior roads too well after years of riding them nearly every day. As she winds round to the path that catches the canal, she briefly exits her own body and sees the seasons of herself appear over the same scene; in gloves and layers of thermals in the winter, leaves almost frozen where they fall; with an itching nose and puffy eyes in spring, flowers singing from the sunken gardens; in a tank top and gym shorts in summer, shoulders and thighs bronzing in real time, past the young lovers and old smokers lolling about on benches with cheap cider from the off-licence rankling in the afternoon sun. And always sweating, whether in darkest frost or most brilliant heat, refusing to let up until her clothes stick to her back, her mouth dries and her legs, drowning in lactic acid, scream at her to stop. This is where she and Enzo always differed; he saw cycling as a leisure activity, but from the outset, she imbued it with fanatical physicality.

The lake has been in so many films and television shows it borders on parody, but that doesn't stop Elly from loving it. It is her spiritual centre point, the place she always chooses to dismount even though it's still a good fifteen-minute ride from her flat. She especially loves arriving there in the morning, at the recently opened Pavilion Bakery and devouring a fresh croissant, the pieces falling all over her black activewear. It is the only time she eats like this, with the abandon of a famished explorer who has finally speared a wild animal. Elly gazes out at the lake, with its wonky fountain and mess of ducks, mallards and swans, and feels at peace. Her heart bangs around her chest. She waits for the sound of Enzo skidding to a stop behind her, the adorable staccato of his panting as he reaches over to snatch the last bite of her pastry.

'Jesus Christ, Babe,' he says, breathless. 'I didn't know we were training for the Olympics.'

**Will Lippington 16.14**
**Hi, is this still available?**

'Brilliant,' Will said, throwing his legs over Roxy and testing her handlebars.

'It's been so hard to find a taller frame, you know. I tried every shop and all the stores online. Did everyone over six foot evacuate town when we left the EU or something?'

Ever since he'd shambled up to the security gate fifteen minutes late, Will gave off the distinct impression of someone whose limbs were still figuring out which direction to go. I could have said the same thing about his hair, messes of straw blond that flopped about and kept getting in his eyes whenever he spoke.

'We just moved back to the city,' Will continued. 'From Australia.'

'That's a big change,' I offered, though he'd already told me this in considerable detail during our message exchange.

'I'd have preferred not to have left, if I'm honest. The quality of life there, it's just . . . you can see why Brits go on holidays and stay for the rest of their lives.'

The more Will gripped Roxy's brakes, the less enthused I was about the prospect of parting with her. He seemed totally normal, but that was half the problem. She deserved to belong to someone exceptional.

'What's her name?'

'Excuse me?'

'Your bike. Does she have a name?'

'Is that something people do, name their bikes?'

'Only if they really love them,' he said, sliding his bony fingers delicately across Roxy's frame. 'This looks like something you love.'

'That's a good observation.'

Judging by his message history, Will was a very excitable man. That he looked more like a second-form boy who'd spent a few nights on a torture rack was beside the point; he was clearly rapt at the idea of finding a bike to replace the one he'd had to leave in Sydney, which he'd told me about in exhaustive and frankly unnecessary detail. Will's Down Under bike had been called Andy, named after his favourite balding tennis champion. He could only ride the thing to and from the beach, he'd explained in a message at 7.08 am two days after I'd already agreed to sell mine to him, because unlike the glorious flatness of London, the city was full of hills that were wholly unforgiving of Andy, his bright blue single-speed with custom white wheels. From this barrage of mostly one-way chat I quickly deduced that Andy was a large part of Will's identity. On the evening before he was to complete the transaction, in spite of the fact that I had left his last twelve messages unread, Will would lay out in great detail the saga of his escape from the Antipodes and the reason Andy had been left behind.

11.19
so basically what happened & I'm sure she won't mind me telling you this bc we don't know each other and will probs never see each other again.

11.21
my sister has been unwell for quite some time. we thought it was a garden variety wobble but now we think it could be postpartum depression or something, she's been getting really down and anxious and it's just my dad over here and he's from that generation where they have no fkn idea what's going on, so he's calling me at like 3 in the morning on the day of a big pitch meeting all like 'your sister has cracked it and I can't handle this do I schedule her or what, I don't rlly know anymore' and to make matters worse my dad types everything in all caps so every time I open my phone I feel like there's an emergency or someone's just died and have a minor heart attack

11.34
sorry I just realised this has nothing to do with buying a bike it's just been very stressful.

11.35
so she's getting worse and won't eat more than a slice of toast, up at all hours of the night,

refuses to go to a&e or a private gp or whatever and it's all just unravelling long distance and it's so bad. sophie (that's my partner btw) is missing the uk anyway, i think she never liked it there as much as me so when we get the call we just pack up our lives in like 72 hours, sell off all our shit and jump on a plane.

11.45
anyway emily is doing a lot better but I had to sell my bike and it's been eating at my soul so this is a long way of saying you're about to make some completely bonkers stranger squatting in camberwell very happy.

11.48
god, what a TLDR. promise I'm not a serial killer. cya tomorrow. sorry.

'So when did you buy him? Or is it –'

'Her. I didn't. She was a gift from my husband. We're separated. Probably divorce soon.'

I was amazed at how easy this was to say after weeks of saying nothing to anyone about it. I hadn't yet told my parents, or my friends. Putting it into words had felt like too much, like I was formally signing a death warrant. Now, without even realising it, this complete random from the internet had won the sad girl lottery.

Will looked forlorn. 'I'm sorry to hear that. We're about to get married, actually. Shit, you probably didn't need to hear that. I'm such a wanker.'

'No it's fine, really. Congratulations. Maybe you can ride Roxy down the aisle.'

'Roxy?'

'Yep.'

'Named after your favourite porn star?'

I snorted laughter, louder than I'd expected to.

'Not far off, you know. But no. After Roxy Music. When I saw that chrome silver I just really thought of '80s glam and like, Bryan Ferry for some reason.'

'Ha! I actually went to uni with Merlin Ferry. Odd guy.'

'Which one is that? I lose count.'

'Youngest. My fiancée says the middle two kids are the best looking.'

By now Will and I had been standing awkwardly in the entry hall for a good fifteen minutes. I could feel the conversation coming to a natural conclusion, but for some reason I wasn't quite ready for it to taper off. While he was the inverse of Enzo in almost every way, Will was still a person, a breathing, feeling organism in a space where there hadn't been anyone else for close to a month. Every one of those days had dragged themselves bare-knuckled across the calendar, marking the time of my self-imposed prison sentence. I walked around the flat in four layers with the heating on, always cold, feeling like there were no doors or walls. It wasn't that I was averse to time spent alone, but after ten years together, I found myself with no idea how to fill the space without him in it, which seemed to grow larger each week. But my own individual identity, which I had recently begun to doubt had ever existed, was affirmed by Will, in all his standard public-school goofiness. He could see me, so I was real. These Marketplace exchanges could well be the only interactions I'd have with anyone outside work for the foreseeable future. Bizarre and strange as they would more than likely prove to be, I felt it was in my best interests to prolong them.

I nudged open the door behind me a bit wider, exposing my flat of soon-to-be-flogged furniture to the world for the first time.

'It's cold out,' I offered, trying desperately to appear normal. 'Fancy a quick cup of tea?'

To his credit, Will had initially appeared unmoved by my recent life excavation. When prompted, he chose the most ridiculous mug we owned, a wraparound that zoomed in on Michelangelo's *David*'s genitalia, which I'd bought immediately upon sighting it during my first trip to Italy with Enzo.

'So I have to stick with Roxy, I take it.'

'Oh absolutely. Did you not see that fine print on the listing? Her name is part of the terms of sale. I know what you look like now, so if you change it, I'll have you murdered.'

'You have people in South London, I presume.'

'There are four Ferry sons. I have someone in every borough.'

'Shame, that.' Will winked, taking a large gulp of tea that I was able to trace down his Adam's apple thanks to his translucent skin. 'I was thinking she'd make a wonderful Merlin.'

'When she's ready to transition I promise you'll be the first to know.'

Will looked around at the flat, noting the glaring spaces where regular furniture was supposed to be, and the jumbled corner where I'd been stacking everything I wanted to sell.

'So, is this like a post-relationship purge or something?'

'Of sorts. I'm not getting rid of everything. Just the stuff that really reminds me of him. Also, I've got to cover rent for two now.'

'Not to be a dick,' he said, 'but when you're together with someone for a while . . . how long?'

'Ten years. Married one.'

'Right, a decade. That's a long time. Doesn't everything remind you of that person? Like, why that couch, table and Roxy, but not the fridge?'

'The fridge came with the flat, and if I sold Lex's Smeg my barely reasonable rent would likely triple overnight.'

'Alright, alright. Bad example. But you know what I mean.'

'I do.'

'Arguably you should just call time on this place and all the negative associations and move out altogether.'

'But I don't only have negative associations. I also have many wonderful ones. Look at these high ceilings and arched windows. I'd be mad to give this place up.'

Tucking his hair behind his ears, Will set his tea down and went to take a proper look around the flat.

'I suppose you're right,' he called from the bathroom. 'Very good for those of amplified stature such as ourselves. Nothing to hit our heads on.'

'A huge bonus, yes,' I called back.

Will re-emerged, holding the only photo frame I'd been unable to throw out.

'Pardon my nosiness, but this man doesn't look very tall.'

'5'7. Or 8 if he stands on his tiptoes, which he does often.'

'Not a good fit for Roxy then,' he mused. 'What does he call his steed?'

'You're going to laugh.'

'I mean, that's what I'm here for. Tragic stories and LOLs.'

'Well he left it behind, but it's much too short for you to ride.'

'You're deflecting. Go on, then. Spill.'

'Andiamo.'

'My Italian isn't that good, but I'm not sure that's a name.'

'It isn't. It means "let's go". But you can only say it with an exclamation mark and both your hands flailing, like this,' I said, puncturing the air in front of me forcefully. 'Andiamo!'

'Ah, I see. Andiamo!'

'More vigour. *Andiamo*!'

'ANDIAMO!' Will roared, provoking hysterical fits of laughter from both of us. It was the first time I'd pissed myself at something in a long time, and I giggled uncontrollably long after the joke had ceased to be funny.

'Maybe stick with Merlin,' I spluttered, setting myself off again in a cataclysm of cackles. 'Seems a good fit.'

'No,' he said, suddenly serious. 'She definitely stays a Roxy.'

*

'How is your sister, anyway?' I was washing up the teacups and plates as Will counted out 300 pounds in cash at Lex's make-shift breakfast bar.

'Emily? Oh, she's doing much better. We got her in with a great psychologist, which took forever, but she's finally started breaking through it. I'm so glad, she was in a really terrible place. Imagine, you make it all the way to the finish line, finally achieve motherhood, and then you get saddled with that for an entire year.'

'I don't know why everyone makes having kids out to be this life-affirming process. It really sets the bar far too high.'

'Oh don't get me wrong; Edie, my niece, is fab. But I agree with you. I feel like if women properly knew even half of this stuff going in, there's no way you or I would have been born.'

'Good thing I was an accident,' I said.

'Like ending up with a short man?'

'Exactly like that.' I dried the last plate and set it aside. 'Are you upset you had to leave Australia?'

'I've sort of rationalised it to myself. We went for a holiday and stayed for three years. All our family is here. It was never going to be forever. But my word, it was incredible. The weather, the food, getting up and surfing every morning before work.'

'Yeah. I sometimes think that's how he felt about Italy, too.'

'Is that why you broke up? He wanted you to ride Roxy and Andiamo around some cobblestoned town forever?'

'Not quite. I think it was a combination of things. God, I loved him so much though. If he walked back through that door and said let's move to some slum in Naples and eat day-old cannoli until we die I think I'd do it in a heartbeat.'

'But instead, you're divesting yourself of all his possessions . . .'

'Our possessions.'

Will laid the towers of twenties in three neat piles.

'Who am I to impart advice? I just bolted on the best country in the world for the sake of someone else's illusion of happiness.'

We walked to the door. I watched as Will wheeled Roxy out towards the courtyard and away from my life forever.

'You compromised,' I said abruptly. 'If we'd compromised, you wouldn't be holding Merlin right now. You wouldn't even be here.'

'Roxy.'

'Merlin.'

'Roxy,' he said firmly.

'Merlin.'

'Roxy, and fuck you.'

The security door buzzed obnoxiously as Will stood at the threshold. We stared each other down for what felt like forever. Lola ran back and forth between the courtyard and hallway, but neither of us paid her any attention.

'Andy,' I said. 'Her name is Andy.'

Tying his stupid floppy hair in a knot, Will smiled as he blinked back tears. 'You know what? Just this once, I'll allow it.'

# INTERMEZZI: GRIME

When Enzo finally moved to London in 2005, after years of being badgered about it by his Florentine university mates, he immediately noticed two things. First, this was not a coffee-drinking country. The closest approximation of coffee was something the English called Caffè Nero, which he made a beeline for as it sounded vaguely like home, only to watch in horror as a disaffected teenager with neon pink braids named Nadia mangled a macchiato within an inch of its life. It was after the ensuing quarrel about how a macchiato was to be prepared, with a small 'stain' of milk (according to the Neapolitan tradition, now at least forty years young), that Enzo, having just been called *wasteman* as he unceremoniously spat the weak, tepid brown liquid into the bin, tripped upon the second thing: there were a lot more English words in London than he had been taught in his uni course.

Over time, he would begin to realise that these were slang terms, of which he knew many in his own language from yelling them at his sisters and cousins. (He would also discover and fall in love with Bar Termini, a safe haven for expat Italians in Soho where one could order an espresso at the bar and not have a violent physiological reaction upon consuming it.) But what fascinated him was how this new lexicon, which seemed to have arisen almost entirely from localised hip-hop and gangs that formed around it and had almost no connection to the Queen's English whatsoever, had squirrelled its way into the national vernacular. Like every teenager who grew up in the MTV generation, he'd seen this happen before. Internationalised versions of 'yo, dawg' and 'wassup?' had long since been parsed into local greetings in his hometown, even though they still showed up nowhere in the dictionary. But the extent and the velocity of it, the way the words danced and ricocheted across sound systems and shopkeepers, TV presenters and cab drivers, morphing itself seemingly every twenty-four hours, well, this was something else entirely.

Enzo's crashlanding into grime arrived care of Kano's 'P's and Q's', a song that served as the perfect entrée to the dizzying and sometimes impermeable complexities of the genre. The first time he heard it was in Topman of all places, lost between floors and searching for a new summer shirt that wasn't hideous. The track was buoyed by crushed gunshot snares, side-chained bass kicks that warped trumpets into something sinister and rapid-fire lyrics that crunched together postcode rivalry, drug slang, street patois and curious

Britishisms. It sent Enzo down an investigative rabbit hole from which he would never truly return. Ever the journalist, he began compiling a notebook of new terms, researching relationships between MCs and slowly, painstakingly, figuring out this whole new world.

It can safely be said that by the time he met Elly, Enzo was the most rabid Italian grime fan in the UK – by a healthy margin. Given his line of work and the circles he mixed in, this was a side of himself that he rarely revealed in public. But as the genre enjoyed its second coming and went global, he started to feel more comfortable showing that he knew his Wileys from his Dizzees, or that he could recite Ghetts and D Double E cyphers from memory without requiring a translator.

Elly discovered Enzo's proclivity for grime relatively early in their relationship, after he reeled off the video clips that had been shot in E8, their neighbourhood. She thought it was cute, in the same way that fifty-year-old women find their husbands' miniature train sets cute. She rarely batted an eyelid if he went out on his own late at night, having read news of an MC clash in Tottenham or Bow on Twitter.

Having grown up with a mother who was equally obsessed with the beats and bass of her time, Elly was well versed in the art of listening to other people explain their deep, almost fanatical love for popular music. Some of her earliest memories had been of her mother trying to convince her dad, often while sloshed, that the Happy Mondays were the next Beatles. Records in her childhood home were only ever played at maximum volume, especially The Smiths, who had formed in Manchester the same year she was born. By comparison, Elly's latent passion for British indie music had formed mostly in private. When she finally escaped to London, she'd already cycled through her goth, rave and shoegaze phases, settling on a broad palate that allowed room for anything that made her feel something. And while grime flew right over her head on a lyrical level, there was something to be said for the sound of it. Punk at its core, devised by outcasts looking in on society, she didn't have to understand it to get it.

As a regular who clearly knew his stuff, Enzo was afforded a tolerance rarely extended to interlopers in the scene. Though this started as casual amusement, a white Italian up the front at illegal raves and mic battles, it eventually took the form of hard-won respect.

Enzo couldn't spit, had never learned to DJ and didn't own a single tracksuit. He continued to show up, no venue too underground or dangerous for his insatiable love for seeing the music in its dank, backroom flesh. Enzo was even bestowed a street name by the rave regulars, Double O-Live, so named for the sheen of his skin.

The year that Elly walked out on him without even leaving the room was a momentous one for grime tragics. Dave's 'Funky Friday' was the number one song in the country. Skepta finally broke America. By the next summer, Stormzy would headline Glastonbury in a bulletproof vest designed by Banksy and you wouldn't be able to go anywhere in England without hearing 'Vossi Bop'. The timing, as it tends to be in these stories, was bittersweet; the moment at which Enzo was finally able to embrace the art form he truly loved was also when he lost the only peng ting he truly loved.

# II. VINYL

ENZO PADS INTO Elly's kitchen, searching for cereal. It's 2011, the last winter they will spend living alone and shuttling between each other's flats at opposite ends of London. Enzo wears nothing but his boxers as he rummages around the pantry that he already knows is going to be empty. Like much of the millennial British workforce, Elly rarely has the time or inclination to use her kitchen. Her fridge consists largely of pickled things, her cupboards all tea bags and tinned tuna. Elly calls these ghosts of groceries 'bits', like she's always on the way to get the rest of what she needs, but the truth is that she hates lingering at home. Her flatmate, Adriana, is an atypically morose Spaniard who is prone to loud groaning and severe eye rolls whenever Elly suggests some form of social activity and mostly stays in her cupboard of a room, repainting her nails, smoking out of her half-open window and watching *Breaking Bad.*

Perennially single by choice, Adriana despises most men and has already written off Enzo, with his enthusiasm and booming voice and insistence on introducing Tortellini Tuesdays into the Hoxton fifth-floor flat, as the enemy.

Enzo is bold by design but would never risk being caught trouserless while Adriana is around. But she is back in Andalusia on her annual pilgrimage to a more temperate winter, so he and his sticky bare legs have the run of the joint.

He is in the process of brewing tea, black for him, regular for Elly, who is taking a shower, when something on the radio catches his ear. Elly has a battered digital box that's made to look endearingly vintage, faux red leather with fake tuning knobs, always fixed to BBC 6 Music. It's Lauren Laverne's morning show, which they both love but usually listen to on playback because by the time she starts they're usually at work. But on this particular gloomy Friday, during this particular February, Enzo is yet to start his new job and Elly has called in sick from her interior design firm so they can spend the day in bed together.

When Elly finally makes it to the kitchen, wringing the last of her hair dry, she finds Enzo rooted to the spot, kettle in hand and mid-pour like someone has attacked him with a real-life pause button. He is still wearing only his underwear, faint goosebumps appearing on the bottom of his thighs. Outside, a skeletal tree braces against the wind. The building rattles in protest. None of that makes it into the room, however, which Enzo has filled with the sound of the radio.

The song is a sketch, yet somehow also fully realised. It is spare synth chords plucked out note by note, playing off against an opening refrain that unfurls like a music box.

*What is this thing?* Enzo wonders as he remains in suspended animation. *What is this thing that is so many beautiful parts at once?* Dubstep ballads are definitely not commonplace in the winter of 2011. That a piece of music can propel itself forward while remaining so limber and delicate is something pretty special.

As always, Elly and Enzo notice things in different ways. It's what makes them such a strong couple, this ability to draw from the same well but find different forms of refreshment. There is no ego. When Elly arrives in the kitchen, what she hears first are the melodies. She knows the female voice immediately. Everyone in East London has heard Jessie Ware by now; she seems to be everywhere that year, showing up on all the biggest club tunes like she's always been there. But there's someone else on the track, this transcendent, soulful melody by someone she can't quite tell the gender of. It could be a woman pitched down, as is in vogue right now, but she realises as it hits the last chorus that it's actually a phenomenally emotive man, with a tremoring, delicate voice like a foghorn. Something about his delivery reminds her of the first time she was exposed to Jeff Buckley. A nerve twitches, deep below her skin, and she shivers reflexively. She is, much like Enzo, completely transfixed.

Love songs can be penned with an audience in mind, but ultimately, it's the lovers that give them meaning. As Elly and Enzo scrub back through the digital stream to listen to the song over and over again, tea turning Siberian in the chipped

Anthropologie mugs with the gold handles that Elly refuses to throw out, this song becomes theirs. Without a single word being spoken, it locks into their hearts like a rare amulet.

It's a freezing February 7th and the song being premiered is called 'Valentine'. As Lauren will remind listeners when she plays it back for a second helping, it's a rare one-off duet from two of the hottest voices in British indie music, performed by Jessie Ware and Sampha – the voice that captured Elly's imagination – both of whom have recently clocked up studio time with the masked wonder known only as SBTRKT. The three collaborators will all work on one another's records over the years but this pair will never record anything like this ever again, a flickering glow-worm in the depths of winter.

Eventually Enzo lets the show run long enough to hear that the trio are releasing the song as a heart-shaped 12-inch vinyl for Valentine's Day.

'The run will be limited to 200 copies, hidden in record stores across the UK,' Lauren announces in her fabulous Northern accent. 'Can't imagine they'll be hanging around for long. Good luck with that, Romeos.'

When Elly, who abhors Valentine's Day as much as Adriana, wakes up to a slim square sleeve wrapped in lurid red crepe paper, she knows better than to ask how or why. Adriana has a shit record player in her room, but Enzo refuses to let her open the packaging. It turns out he wants to frame it for their new flat, which they haven't even found yet but which he imagines will be somewhere close by, so he'll never have to commute from dreary Archway again.

'It's not a piece of art,' Elly laughs, throwing scrunched up tissue paper at him across the table. 'It's a record. It's designed to be played.'

'Okay, primo, non è vero. Of course it is art, Babe. You have heard this song. It is . . . transcendente.'

'So you don't want to hear it ever again?'

'Of course, of course, but we have internet, Spotify. We can hear whenever we want.'

'Enzo,' she says, running her fingers around the outline of the stone-grey record with its candy, heart-shaped pink label, 'I love you but honestly, you're completely mad.'

'True,' he replies. 'I am mad for you.'

The framed record is the first thing to go up on the wall after they move into Academy Apartments. Their landlord, Lex, who is an actual record producer, finds it completely hilarious – especially Enzo's added inscription.

'If you want some more of these, I've got plenty gathering dust in my studio,' he jokes when he comes to fix the hot water for them one afternoon. 'Good song, though. Nice production.'

But Lex knows better than most that it's only the songs that make you freeze that end up behind glass. Lovers give love songs meaning, after all.

'Valentine' remains in suspended animation for the next seven years.

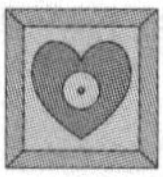

**Xenia Parish 03.08**
**Hi, is this still available?**

I could hear Xenia before she even got to the first outside gate. She had to be about 80 per cent bracelets. Everything seemed to bounce off her; beads, crystals, charms, necklaces, earrings, nose rings, ringlets, even light itself. Opening the door to let her in was a bit like being punched in the face by a pack of Skittles, an overwhelming rush of technicolour. If this sounds like a lot, what's worse is how good Xenia appeared to be at throwing these conflicting shades together. She should have looked like a deranged children's entertainer; instead, she came off like an honorary member of Hot Chip.

Xenia bounded through the door, yellow crop top and purple flares, neon orange Cons and the aquamarine tint of what looked like a bellybutton piercing. It would have still been alright, I think, if the first words out of that perfectly oval mouth weren't –

'Babe, this place is like, next-level incredible . . .'

She wasn't to know what the word meant to me, but I started crying anyway. It was so facile and the more I willed myself to stop, the worse it became, until I was face down on the couch, pushing out those pathetic, lonely owl hoots that I usually only allowed myself when I was alone. Months later, still a complete fucking mess. Writing texts and deleting them. Downloading dating apps, instantly matching with a bunch of absolutely gross men whose pictures had them holding fish or worse, babies, and immediately deleting them.

Calling but hanging up before the line connected. Mining the people I knew who knew people Enzo knew for small morsels of information about how he was faring. Dialling tarot reader hotlines from the back pages of *Metro*, passive-aggressively forwarding joint invites to weddings, birthdays and christenings to his work email. Buying a spenny new black Moleskine and spending long evenings scribbling about how I'd suicide-bombed my own love life and any chance at future happiness. Considering a rescue dog, before remembering that I already technically co-owned a cat.

The predictability of it was what upset me the most. Everyone had seen this film before. It was boring. Xenia soon located the tissues, and after I recovered, I gave her a potted history of the implosion of my relationship. I really hadn't banked on reliving the trauma with every bloody person who came to pick something up, but I'd forgotten that in this case, the item in question came with a personalised inscription.

More people had tried to buy the record than anything else I'd put up on Marketplace. My inbox was a swamp of obsessive music enthusiasts, the kind I had once found endearing but who were now mostly annoying. They came at me at all hours with their highly specific Discogs questions, asking about plastic shrink wrapping and sleeve condition, pressings, editions and locations. Enzo had clearly been right to hunt down that 12-inch when he had; judging from the interest, they were now extremely hard to come by. Some chap whose body odour I could imagine just from the ardent frequency of his enquiries offered me £600 for it – almost as much as we'd paid for our dining room table.

It was so exhausting I considered turning my notifications off entirely, except I still had all the other stuff to sell. That's probably what made me decide on Xenia, in addition to the fact that she was the least obnoxious crate digger and a bona fide DJ. She was also the only girl.

The problem with the vinyl was that I didn't really want to get rid of it, at least, not as much as some of the other gear I was offloading, but I also couldn't bear having the damn thing in the house. I tried taking it off the wall and hiding it, but I could still feel its presence, pulsing out from whichever dark upstairs nook I'd shoved it in. This perfect two minutes of music, pressed onto a format we couldn't even play because we were both too lazy to invest in a proper record player, was one of many unexplainable totems of a decade-long romance I now found myself having to justify to someone I'd never met.

Mercifully, Xenia didn't have long to hang around and chat. Through both her sartorial decisions and her general demeanour, she struck me as someone who could move seamlessly between multiple subcultures, a raver who was also in a rock band, a wellness evangelist partial to biblical benders. This at least somewhat explained her outfit choice, which encompassed almost every colour swatch known to mankind – and a few we hadn't discovered yet. While I was attempting to reverse-Frankenstein the story of why we'd had this record framed, her phone lit up about 2000 times. I realised quickly that the only thing I could safely assume about Xenia was that she was popular. I'd never trusted popular people. They always wanted something from you.

'Obviously I feel terrible,' she said as I led her over to the stairs, where the still-encased record was once again hanging on the wall. I'd given it a quick dust so that the gold of the personalised plate mounted below the 12-inch practically glowed.

'Why's that?'

'I mean, I'm going to have to break the glass.'

'I should hope so. How else are you going to play it?'

She peered closer.

'It's just so beautiful, the inscription. I feel like I'm shattering some sort of deep, cosmic love egg and it's going to ooze its life force out into the universe. I'll be personally responsible, you know?'

'Wow. Do you always talk like that?'

'Like what?'

'Like you've swallowed a stack of crystals and you've got a jade egg shoved up your arse for good measure.'

She smiled. 'I've never thought about it. There isn't really a methodology to my speech; I guess I'd put it down to my deliberate, conscious relationship with the subtle earthly vibrations that exist all around us.'

'You're doing it again.'

'I'm fucking with you, Elly. It's a means to an end, just like everything else in our lives. Like, did you always wear all black or was that just when you moved to London?'

'Always.'

'So when you were three, you specifically asked your mum to dress you like Wednesday Addams?'

'To be honest, I just sort of channelled my place in the stardust we call existence and realised my internal aura was something much darker.'

She laughed. 'See? It's not that hard. And if it helps my clients, why not?'

'Nothing wrong with a bit of light theatre.'

'Give the people what they want.'

'You know,' I said, finding where the string connected to the nail in the wall and delicately pulling the record down, 'I just had a thought. You could smash the frame at the end of one of your sets.'

'Ooh. Very avant-garde.'

'I mean, tell the story if you want. The cosmic egg and all that.'

'Babe, I barely know the story.'

'You're going to have to stop calling me that,' I said.

'Babe?'

'Yeah.'

'I call everyone babe, though. Even my boss.'

'I've no doubt.'

My change in tone seemed to convince Xenia that I was serious.

'Alright, alright, I can do this. Maybe I can call you Wednesday.'

'Maybe you can just call me Elly.'

'Less fun, I'll admit, but also a good suggestion.'

'I don't think I ever want anyone to say that to me again.'

'The B-word?'

'See? You're learning.'

Like many of the people crowding out my inbox, Xenia had been searching for the song for a long time. It was, as she described it, a cleansing closer, which made more sense when you considered what her live sets were designed for. When she wasn't working as a stringer for a press wire service, filing stories about child rebel soldiers in her honey-smoked, indiscernible accent that could be derived from any number of Eastern European countries, Xenia ran sound baths. Deploying the skills she'd learned DJing in clubs in her twenties, she mixed transcendental ambient synths with gongs, chimes, chanting and other sound sources that she swore occurred naturally around Peckham Rye. For the privilege of this 45-minute immersion, customers paid Xenia 20 quid upon entering. On a good Wednesday, when she ran two sessions each comprising around thirty to forty people, she made enough to cover rent on the studio she barely slept in and a new set of candy beads every week.

'It's like taking a trip to the Amazon, by way of Philip Glass,' she explained.

'Humid and repetitive?'

'Definitely,' she said, sidestepping the joke. 'You don't want a cold room. Bad for internal circulation.'

'So where does "Valentine" fit in this zonked-out rainforest?'

'I always like to end the set on a song that has lyrics. It helps bring everyone back to the room. But you need it to fit aesthetically with what's come before it, to flow through, which is the hard part. Folk music doesn't really work, and if I can avoid Moby, I will at all costs.'

'Don't pretend you were too cool for Moby back in the day,' I said.

'Don't pretend you still listen to him,' she shot back.

'Fair play. But why does it have to be vinyl? You're not making life easy for yourself.'

'I have to use the best possible audio quality I can find. When your eyes are closed and there's nothing to distract you, you can really hear how streaming strips everything out from a track. Also, people are paying to be there. It's a journey. If they wanted to just play stuff off their phones, they could do that at home.'

'I see. Well, it's a good choice. I've always loved the song.'

'It sounds like floating.'

'I suppose it does.'

'Honestly, the first time I heard it I emailed my friend who works at NTS Radio like a hundred times to find out what it was.'

'It was very special to us, too, like I said. I'm glad it's going to someone who will appreciate it.'

'No word of a lie, tracking down records like this is why I do what I do. Everyone thinks sound baths are just for meditation, but mine are also made to be cathartic. You need to feel something dislodge inside you and slowly wash away, or I ain't doing my job right.'

I hadn't considered a world in which listening to 'Valentine' again wouldn't be horrendously painful. Briefly, I tried to picture myself lying in a humid room of anonymous bodies, experiencing the song anew. I could just about make out my face, but not the expression written on it.

Xenia had summoned a joint from somewhere deep within her mess of blonde ringlets. I didn't want to know how long it had been there. She picked up the frame with her free hand and tucked it beneath her arms.

'I'm going to go burn this, but you should come to the bath. It's next Wednesday, under the arches at London Fields.'

'Everything's under the arches at London Fields. Be a bit more specific.'

'You'll feel the energy.'

'Oh, piss off then,' I said, palming her notes and shoving them in my wallet. 'I'll try and make it. Never even seen that record out of its sleeve, have I?'

I was late. I'd guessed – incorrectly – that Xenia would be running the sound bath out of a ready-made space beneath the arches, like the pop-up cinema or that basement venue that hosted ratchet festival afterparties and changed both names and owners every six months. But both were completely dark. As I paced up and down Mentmore Terrace, breathing out frosty air and trying to figure out where the fuck I was supposed to be, I heard what sounded like pan flutes coming from somewhere nearby. Following my ears, I found myself outside e5 Bakehouse, which made absolutely no logical sense until I pushed open the door.

Most of my afternoon had been wasted composing and deleting an email to Enzo, because texting seemed too intimate and a phone call was absolutely out of the question. It had proven annoyingly difficult. The idea was to burn enough time typing and hitting backspace on various permutations of 'I fucking love you, I'm terrified, please come home' that I'd pass the point of no return at which it would be too late to go to the sound bath. Unfortunately, Xenia was extremely eager. She'd not only messaged me on Marketplace but also called to remind me of the date, while conveniently forgetting to tell me where I was actually meant to be going, somehow intuiting that she'd piqued my curiosity enough to coax me out of the flat in the thickness of my misery. She'd also put me on the door, arguably the greatest injustice, as there'd now be a clear record of whether I'd shown up. 'If you're on the list, you must go,' Enzo had said to me once when I asked him why he was trekking out to a show in West London on an absolutely freezing Thursday evening, 'or you never invited back again.'

With the tables, chairs and racks all pushed to the sides, the room was significantly bigger than I remembered it being during the day. There were yoga mats and blankets laid out in equal increments and they covered the space from wall to wall, row upon row stretching from the door to the corridor that led to the actual bakery, where Xenia had set up a makeshift DJ booth on the service counter, covered in dark purple fabric. It appeared she'd found a way to jack into the cafe's not-insignificant sound system, filling the cavernous semicircle with warmth and sound. Bodies, too, dozens of them, lay supine on their mats, surrendering to this sonic tour. The flutes changed to crashing waves over a low drone: gulls. Between cueing up records, Xenia spied me lurking sheepishly in the corner and waved, pointing to a spare mat.

I'd never been a fan of mat-related activities. They reinforced my longstanding suspicion that I was just too tall, my head jutting out onto the cold floor or my arms bumping into other people. You never feel more gangly than when getting up and down off the floor. Settling onto the thin foam, I tried not to think about how ungainly and disproportionate I was. I closed my eyes and imagined what Enzo would say if he saw me here among the East London trustafarians. He'd likely have a fit.

Xenia wasn't an amateur. Her changes were seamless, the set flowing effortlessly between transportive and meditative, and during an extended spell of repeated chiming bells, my guard completely broke down. I'd spent so many years listening to mp3s and streaming music through Bluetooth headphones, so many winters cuddling on the couch instead of clubbing that I'd forgotten what it was like to be totally swaddled in sound. It was hard to remain self-conscious in a space where nothing was expected of me but to lie there and absorb vibrations. It struck me, amid a sea of other sudden revelations, that it had been a long while since I'd listened to music with any sort of intent. I was so zoned out that I barely noticed the hour go by, or that Xenia had dipped into her vinyl carrier bag to pull out our 'Valentine', free from its glass cage and ready to feel a needle pressed into its grooves for the very first time. The room had become steadily darker as the session had progressed, but now Xenia slowly turned the light back up as she brought the bath to an end. I heard the opening salvo even as she was still mixing out of the track before it. The flutters, the feeling. Weightlessness. I breathed in. Everything smelled of bread. The heaviness of the moment fell onto me. My ribcage was about to crack open.

'Is called arpeggio,' I heard Enzo say through the mist.

'Arpeggio?'

'Si,' he said proudly, as he did whenever he taught me anything Italian. 'A chord, but in notes. Like this.'

I watched as he played an imaginary piano in the air, punctuating each note.

'It's beautiful.'

'And when you repeat arpeggio, it become ostinato.'

'Alright professor,' I said, kissing his nose. 'That's enough class for today.'

In high definition, on proper speakers, in the arched room, 'Valentine' shimmered in a completely different way. I'd never heard it like this, and I'd listened to it hundreds, maybe thousands of times. Xenia was right; in this setting, the song took on a different dimension. It was rich and deep. The rhythm effects were insects; Sampha crooned directly in my ear. The bass sucked open a hole in the floor, a ripple in time, and I fell through it.

There's only so long you can cling to two minutes. Or ten years.

When I opened my eyes, the room was close to empty. A few stragglers were helping roll up the mats. Most of the participants used the final song of the session as a chance to pack up, stretch, wriggle back into their coats and head for the door. It was a small victory; the song had been played for everyone in the bath but had only impacted me. I'd given it away, but it was still mine.

I sat cross-legged in my post-bathing stupor, wondering if this was one of those things nobody told you about adult relationships. It seemed important, like something I could grab and hold firmly with my fingers. None of my stuff mattered; I could sell it all, pack up shop, move to Stockholm and shack up with a Skarsgård. The story of 'Valentine', goose pimples by the radio in Hoxton, falling in love with something external to one another at precisely the same moment, would still follow me to the ends of the Earth.

Xenia had been hovering by the booth, chatting to some of the last to leave. Now she came over to me, clenching something tightly in her hand. I didn't have to ask what it was. At last, I could see why she was so popular. She remembered what was important.

She'd carefully removed the gold plate from the frame, filled in the holes from the screws and polished it within an inch of its life. It gleamed under the electric lamps of London Fields as I slowly made my way home. Every so often I uncurled my frozen fingers, just to check it was still there, before burying it deep in my coat pocket.

I had to hand it to Xenia. Only she could figure out a way to give me back something I wouldn't be able to sell.

> *I am mad for you, always.*
> *14 February 2011*

# III. TABLE

Whoever said height doesn't matter when you're horizontal clearly hadn't tried to fuck on the edge of Elly's eight-seater, solid timber dining table. After close to three years of secret shagging, apologetic notes to roommates on fridge doors, sneaking in, tiptoeing out and playing the first few Foals albums (lots of shouting, constant, driving rhythm) unnecessarily loud at 2 am, she and Enzo were understandably elated to finally have a space all to themselves.

Most couples would seize the opportunity to decorate said space to their liking, to fill the cupboards with food they didn't need to claim via pass-ag Sharpie scrawls, or cook ridiculous three-course meals on a Tuesday for the hell of it. But for Elly and Enzo, the first order of business was to have sex in every room and on every surface in the flat, which brings us to the infamous dining table.

Enzo, as it has already been noted, was not blessed with Elly's stature but certainly eclipsed her when it came to unbridled enthusiasm. For while fornicating everywhere from the stairs to the windowsill was originally Elly's idea, her mind more creatively attuned to the notion of kinks as a challenge, she was also the first to admit defeat, especially when faced with the issue of basic physics that would not allow for any form of penetration thanks to the table's unusual height – which, it should also be noted, had suited Elly just fine until she'd attempted to do something other than eat off it.

It was also only nominally Elly's table; they had bought it together on a trip to Italy and shipped it home at great expense, but at that point she already held the lease on a flat while he barely had a kettle, so it made sense that she should store and make use of it in the interim. Lord knows it had caused enough grief getting it up her tiny stairwell, the Pickfords lads swearing more than their usual every other word as they fruitlessly tried to bend a solid 2.4-metre piece of wood around the aggressively angled landings.

They loved that fucking table, and there's surely nothing more romantic than making love on top of something you love. It would sadly become the Park Lane of their coital Monopoly board, something they tried to land every so often before admitting it was probably impossible. On one occasion, Enzo retrieved a mini stepladder that he used to access the higher shelves in the kitchen, but Elly was immediately turned off by the prospect and shut it down. She maintained that a simple 'from behind' approach would instantly solve the issue, but he maintained that they could do that anywhere and besides, it was changing the rules.

They'd come across their future fornication furniture in the back streets of Florence, where they'd stopped over for Enzo's ten-year university reunion before heading to Naples to introduce Elly to his parents and absurdly large extended family. Elly, an only child of divorced parents with one first cousin who she'd already decided was a creep by age eleven, was not at all prepared for this Neapolitan onslaught, but figured she probably never would be and besides, she was flat broke and Enzo's parents insisted on paying. As a bonus, she got to spend a week in *Firenze*, as Enzo sternly insisted she pronounce it, a genuine interior designer's fantasy land.

Elly knew that being introduced to the family was a big deal, especially if they didn't like you. Her last serious boyfriend, Ian, had made a point of parading her in front of his mother and brothers within two months of them being together. Their attempts at small talk had petered out before supper had even been served, and she'd spent subsequent visits to their droll house in Brentford in relative silence, half-listening to the three boys bantering incessantly over Arsenal's recent match performances like she wasn't even in the room. Perhaps it was a by-product of her dysfunctional childhood, but Elly didn't see the express need for any additional family in her life. If she were to marry Enzo, which seemed increasingly likely, it would be because of her love for him, not his thirteen first cousins. However, she could not in good conscience say this to the darling boy of a large brood, and so attempted instead to invoke the spectre of their recent mid-year resolutions, in which they'd promised each other to start saving money, be less impulsive and plan for the future, whatever that looked like. Unfortunately, she'd forgotten that this had also been determined to begin after August.

Against the warm light of the laptop, Enzo's eyes sparkled with good humour. 'Is like you always say, Babe. Next year! We are still young, and no children yet. So we enjoy the time, no? And summer in Firenze I promise is bellissima.'

Enzo had found them an apartment off Piazza Santo Spirito, where kids came to drink wine on the steps and smoke cigarettes late into the night. It was ringed by family-run pizza restaurants only the locals seemed to know about, being on the less touristy side of the River Arno, which suited Elly, frequently embarrassed by her own kind while on holiday, just fine. They spent the week in a sort of parallel dreamland, away from their jobs and the internet, rising late, drinking too many one-Euro standing espressos, buying salumi and cheese from the markets and devouring them in the forecourt of yet another famous cathedral, smoking for the hell of it and going to house parties with Enzo's friends, all of whom spoke impeccable English.

Seeing Enzo in his element affirmed Elly's love for him, something she'd been keeping at arm's length without quite knowing why. In the tiny cobblestoned streets, inside the Uffizi or simply ordering gelato, he radiated positive vibrations. It was difficult for an already infectious man to beat his own high score, but having him introduce her to every shopkeeper he'd ever met in that beautiful language she'd made absolutely no attempt to learn really sealed the deal.

Maybe it was that lingering halo that led them to buy their first household item together in another country, despite not yet having made a move to find a place of their own. It was going to be a good sunset, Enzo had said, so they were on their way to Piazzale Michelangelo to toast it with olives and a sixpack of Moretti. Walking through the backstreets by the Boboli Gardens, Elly had spied a store she hadn't seen yet. It looked strangely modern among all the old buildings, and she crossed the street without looking, suddenly intrigued.

The showroom was expertly lit and completely white. It was a relatively large space with only a handful of items in it; two tables, a few chairs and a bizarrely large LED digital clock, which a card informed visitors was not for sale. There seemed to be nobody manning the store at all. By the time Enzo dodged a sudden afternoon rush of scooters to join her, Elly was already gliding her palms along the larger of the tables.

'This is incredible,' she said. 'It looks like a single piece of timber.'

'Si, yes, very beautiful.'

'I've never seen anything like it. I mean, I have, but not in this colour. That texture, it's just . . .'

'What?'

'Well, I haven't looked at the tag and I'm not sure I want to.'

Enzo found the price and did some quick maths.

'Okay, so in pounds, is about 3000. 2800 I think.'

'Christ, 2800 pounds?'

'I mean, yes, but you say yourself. It's designer. It's very high quality.'

'Forget it. There's no point buying something like that.'

'Why not?'

'Well, for one I can't afford it. Not even remotely. Also, there's the slight problem of how shit my flat is and what would a piece like this be doing in a tip like that?'

The shop assistant, who looked exactly as Elly had imagined he would with his steel-framed oval glasses and double denim, had quietly materialised in the corner. He nodded to them with barely perceptible interest.

'I think you should buy it.'

'Darling, no.'

'Look, this whole trip so far cost nothing, right?'

'So you want me to take advantage of your mother's kindness to buy an expensive dining table.'

'No,' he laughed. 'I want you to buy it for you.'

'I don't even have that many friends. This is what, a six-seater?'

'Eight, actually,' the assistant called from the other side of the room. 'It's the last one so we are including the chairs in the total price.'

Enzo whistled through his teeth as he picked up one of the steel dining chairs.

'Babe, this is a good deal.'

'This isn't like your Asos philosophy, you know. It's not bonus money I have just because I got it back. You write about finance, for Christ's sake.'

'Okay,' he said. 'You're right. Another idea.'

Elly laughed. 'There's another idea?'

'We buy together.'

She stared at him.

'Together? You live in a genuine shoebox . . .'

'But you don't. We buy together, it stays in your flat and when we move in together it is our table.'

'Did you come up with this just now? I have to hand it to you, this is next level, even for you.'

'Babe, come,' he said, clasping her hands. 'You always say you want us to find a place for ourselves. We'll never find a table this good for this price in London. Perchè no? It's an investment.'

Elly was listening closely but also trying to stop a rising bubble of anxiety that was surfacing just beneath her clavicle. It was proving difficult to do both effectively at once, and she was tearing up involuntarily at the effort.

'An investment! In what exactly?'

'Well, us, no? We are our future.'

'Sorry to interrupt,' double denim said, suddenly behind them, 'but we have to close in five minutes.'

Elly's mind flickered.

'Are you open tomorrow?'

'Sorry, no. Sunday.'

She always preferred it when her hand was forced. It was much easier to make out later like it wasn't her fault.

'Well,' she sighed, 'I guess we'll be taking it then.'

She slapped Enzo on the butt as he and the owner haggled over shipping.

'Good thing I'm getting it half price.'

**Himesh Varghese 18.43**
**Hi, is this still available?**

Never in my life had I witnessed such a crestfallen man. Having arrived a good half-hour late, Himesh now paced circles around my flat, audibly distressed. Most likely he was berating himself for not asking some obvious questions during our brief online triage. Beyond us sat the table in question; stunning, stoic and, without a shadow of a doubt, far too heavy to be dragged out of my place by an average-sized man and me, an extremely disinterested woman.

'Fuck,' he whistled, 'it's just so *big*.'

'I did say to bring someone with you. In my post? The one you answered?'

'I know, I just thought . . . you know what, I've no idea what I was thinking. Steel legs, too. Christ on a bike . . .'

'Yeah, it's a solid piece of kitchen kit. No returns, obviously.'

'I'm not sure it would even fit in the van, you know.'

'Now, that's not strictly true. Your only issue is how you're going to get it out the door.'

'This is the problem with Marketplace,' he said, exasperated.

'Objects on the internet may be larger than they appear?'

'And heavier . . .'

Himesh methodically examined the table, as if some slight scratch rather than its significant girth was somehow going to influence his purchasing decision. He moved from corner to corner, stooping down to bring the tabletop to eye level and cocking his head to one side. It almost made me believe that he vaguely knew what he was doing.

'Sonja and I, we look after my parents,' he said, continuing his inspection. 'They're getting too old to live by themselves and the rest of our family is back in India. Our table, it's fine, but it's getting pretty cramped, and my girls are almost big enough to sit and have dinner with us now.'

'You know, it's odd; I never really imagined it as a family dining table.'

'How is that possible?' He laughed, gesturing at the expanse of dark wood between us. 'Look at the size of this thing.'

'I mean, it makes sense, clearly. It's just not what crossed our minds when we bought it.'

Of course, this wasn't strictly true. If I hadn't known exactly what Enzo meant when he called the table an investment in our future, the next ten days spent at his parents' apartment in Vomero had left little ambiguity. Everything in the Esposito household centred around the kitchen and, more specifically, their gigantic, expandable table. At least twice a day, anywhere between fifteen to twenty of Enzo's immediate family – cousins, grandparents, toddlers – would swarm in from their neighbouring homes high up in the hills of Naples and sit down to eat, drink and yell over each other. I had been drastically unprepared for this level of continuous, invasive interaction. Sassy siblings pinched my waist, while a rabble of aunts passed open judgement on whether my tits would even hold enough milk. Their kids stared at me like I had landed from another planet.

My hair frizzed dry the second I walked out of the shower, and I spent much of the time fanning myself, likely adding to the idea that I was some dainty princess Enzo had rescued from Olde England.

This makes it sound like they were all utterly mad – which they were – but they could also be quite charming. Enzo's father clocked my discomfort early and would often make some vague pretext to walk out to the balcony with me, where he could smoke and we could watch ships arriving in the Bay of Naples without having to say a word. His younger sister, Sofia, always had another question about the Arctic Monkeys for me. And even the more vicious ones, the bitter, divorced and drunk, who saved their best English to tell rude stories about the girls Enzo had carried home on the back of his scooter over the years, saw how their golden boy doted upon me. By the end of our stay, they were showing me their secret family ragù recipes, the meagreness of my breasts all but forgiven.

Lying in our airless bedroom in Vomero, listening as the funiculars crawled up and down the hillside like exhausted caterpillars, I finally understood why Enzo had been so fixated on paying the balance on the table back in Florence. All I'd seen was a statement piece that we could host real dinner parties around. I had visions of matching denim napkins, Japanese ceramics and expensive wine that other people brought in exchange for a few hours in our exclusive company. But Enzo clearly imagined something very different. Snoring quietly beside me, he dreamed of little hands grabbing another bowl of spaghetti, sauce spilling onto the dark wood. The scraping of chairs after lunch before another game of football in the courtyard. Visits from relatives bearing presents for the bambini, long lunches beneath our big open windows in the spring. It would have been an ideal time to talk about it. The problem, as always, was that I didn't yet have the right words.

'In Italy, right?' Himesh was saying. 'That much I remember from the listing.'

I nodded as he smoothed his delicate hands over the surface, slowly and deliberately.

'I thought it was a prank when Sonja showed me the post. Craftsmanship like this, you just can't find it here. Unless you're a millionaire.'

'If you can believe it, that's why I bought it. Well, why we bought it, anyway. My husband and me. I'm in design. It was an aesthetic decision.'

'Nothing wrong with that, it's a beautiful piece. But tell me something, if I'm not overstepping . . .'

'Not yet.'

Himesh smiled.

'This is an eight-seater. That's a huge commitment on size alone, not to mention cost, for a married couple with no kids.'

'Separated.'

'You've separated?'

'Yes, which is why you're here to take it off my hands. It's obscene for two people, but rather tragic for one, wouldn't you say?'

Himesh seemed more upset at this revelation than I was. He pulled out two of the powdered steel chairs from under the table, gesturing for me to take one. For a while we sat in silence, unsure where to go next.

'I can't buy this from you,' he said eventually. His tone had changed. It felt softer, more tentative.

'Listen, I know it's heavy as all hell, but if you come back later with your wife, I think the three of us could just about manage it. I'll get Oli from next door to help us with the faff of all the security doors.'

Himesh shook his head.

'A separation, it's not always final. The two of you could find a way back . . .'

'That's very sweet, Himesh, but unlikely. We'd probably already be divorced if I wasn't so pathetic and would just start the bloody paperwork. It's over.'

'People change their minds,' he continued, almost trance-like. 'They wake up in a cold sweat at two in the morning and realise they've made a mistake.'

What a sanctimonious bell end.

'Right, but what if there's no mistake? One party holds a particular view or decides to do something that the other can't stomach. Not a fuck-up, or an error. A calculation.'

Himesh drummed his fingers softly on the table as he thought on it. The thick gold of his wedding band caught the fading light from beyond the window, refractions bouncing across the ceiling.

'You're talking about sabotage.'

'That's quite a loaded term, Himesh.'

'A bit like "separation"?'

'It implies there was an element of planning.'

'Didn't you call it a calculation a few seconds ago?'

'Yes, and not to get into semantics because it's starting to get late, but making a calculation is a tad different to being calculating. Like, if I told you that I was going to give you 10 per cent off this table if you paid in cash, you'd do a split-second calculation to figure out if it was worth it.'

'So was it worth it?'

While I stared Himesh down, I took him in properly for the first time. He was quite attractive, in a scruffy, A24 film sort of way. And young, definitely younger than me, despite his apparent sagacity. I wouldn't have put him at much past twenty-seven.

'We reached an impasse. When I couldn't find a way around it, he left. Left me here, with this gigantic slab of wood that we were supposed to own together for the rest of our lives.'

'He could still come back.'

'I'd rather he didn't. Soon there won't be anywhere for him to sit.'

Himesh scanned the room, eyes landing on the Chesterfield against the far wall.

'That's going too?'

'Do you want to do a double?' I joked. 'You might need to fly in some family members to help you get it all in the van.'

'Think I'll stick with the obnoxious tree on legs, thanks. Are you going to move out?'

'No. I love it here. Half of this sale is going straight to the rent.'

'So what, you flog everything and just sit on milk crates feeling sorry for yourself?'

'Once I get rid of it all, everything that reminds me of us, I'm going to give myself a couple of months runway before I go out and buy ludicrously expensive designer pieces that cripple my bank account but bring me small bursts of joy.'

'Right. So if . . . if he does come back one evening, just rings the buzzer and says, "You know, I've thought about that split-second calculation you made a few months ago, and on reflection, I can handle it, it's not enough for me to give up on this marriage," he's going to waltz in here and it's going to look like a totally different flat.'

'Practically unrecognisable. In fact, that's exactly why I'm doing all this, inviting strange men off Facebook into my home to grope my worldly possessions and haggle with me, on the off chance my husband might suddenly materialise without warning, having revised his entire value system, to get the absolute shock of his poor life when he sees all our stuff is gone. Oh, and then Ashton Kutcher jumps out from behind that pot plant over there with a full camera crew, pointing and laughing at him.'

'Ashton who?' Himesh looked blank.

I mimed banging my head violently against the table.

'Himesh, how old are you?'

'I'm twenty-four.'

'Jesus. No wonder you don't know what *Punk'd* is.'

'Age is not important. Why are you so determined that your relationship is over?'

'Why are you so convinced that it isn't?'

We glowered at each other, deadlocked. For a quick second, I thought this might be the moment I broke my post-Enzo drought, but then I remembered why Himesh had come for the table. He also seemed like he wasn't yet ready to leave. I really did know how to pick them.

'Is there somewhere you can smoke around here?' he said, finally. 'I've been stuck in an edit all day and my brain is fiending for nicotine.'

'There's a courtyard in the middle of the building,' I said, packing up my limbs and stretching my back as I got up. Everything cracked. We'd been sitting for far too long. 'Give me a minute to get some boots on and I'll come with you.'

Of the many fantastical aspects of a complex as sprawling as Academy Apartments, I'd always had a soft spot for the courtyard. It wasn't that it was particularly pretty; most cement slabs masquerading as school playgrounds typically aren't. What it did offer, however, was the unique vantage point from which to be able to gawp into the windows of strangers' flats without requiring justification. The basement, first and second levels in the building's inner ring were almost completely visible from the yard, offering design obsessives like yours truly the chance to glimpse the kind of effortlessly chic interiors that only came with having a great eye or too much money. It was a significant achievement to score a flat in here at all, but one could always aspire to be better.

When the weather was warm enough, Enzo and I would stroll out after dinner with our tumblers of wine or cups of tea and look shamelessly into the types of dining and kitchen arrangements that I'd only ever seen in catalogues that came with embossed, bone-coloured business cards. Together, we took mental notes of the various furnishings we would buy straight off the showroom floor when we were rich; that industrial light fixture, those velvet armchairs in forest green, all those hanging plants. I was never sure Enzo really cared how our place looked; his desires always seemed to be more functional. But I loved that he indulged me, listening attentively as I pointed out key pieces, whistling low when I told him how much an original cost.

'Whatever you want, you will have it,' he said, wrapping his arms around my torso as we walked back to our flat. 'But don't worry, when we have a big family, we'll live in a house.'

Some of the flats had mood lighting that switched on in the evenings, bathing the L-shaped courtyard in an orange and magenta glow. I'd never noticed them before, clearly having been too concerned with perving on other tenants' couches and kitchen islands. Himesh seemed more structurally impressed, craning his neck to try and compute how many dwellings were in this one building.

'Incredible,' he said, offering me a cigarette. 'How many people live here? A thousand?'

'I've honestly no idea. It's a bloody city. And it connects to another block the same size, so it could genuinely be that many. There's no central register. We have a Facebook group, but that only covers this wing. None of us really know.'

Himesh took a long drag and gazed up at the flat on the fourth floor that pulsed purple light.

'It's like, I don't know how exactly to put it . . . an elegant slum?'

'I wouldn't say every flat here is stuffed with posh people, but there's a fair bit of trust fund money about. My husband used to call it a freelancer's paradise. You never see half this lot go to work.'

'An estate for the professional services industry, maybe.'

'See? That didn't take long.'

In the distance, I could hear Lola mewling. No matter where she was among the sprawl of the school halls, she always knew when I was out here at night. Soon she'd tiptoe into view, unlikely to be put out by the appearance of a stranger. To live in a building like Academy Apartments was to never fully know who belonged and who was just passing through. It was its own walled city, a bit like Lucca, where Enzo had taken me once and we'd had ended up having a huge fight after we missed the only train back to Florence. It wasn't my fault. I'd told him it was a hair wash day.

We stood in silence, inhaling, exhaling, ashing. Himesh rubbed his beard. I could tell he was considering telling me something important. I had no idea how regular men ever won poker matches with all their blatant physical cues. Just like Himesh, they also opened their mouths to speak on average three to four times before actually saying anything. Like they were testing out the configuration of syllables. Like they'd lost the words somewhere between their brain and their throat.

'I've gone through a separation,' he said, carefully. 'With Sonja. We got together too young, and we hadn't had time to figure out who we were. My career was going tits up, we'd just moved in together and it wasn't working. We expected to be in a better place, I think, after uni. So she started going out and messing around on me. I didn't blame her. Twenty-one is too soon.'

'Was it . . .'

'Were you going to say "arranged marriage"?'

'Er, I . . .'

'My parents love Sonja, but I'm not sure they would have chosen her for me. For a start, she's Muslim.'

'Right.'

'I'm second generation British. My friends and I, we're not really into all that, you know, conceptually. But my brother had an arranged marriage – he's five years older than me. They moved back to India, down south by the sea. Kerala. Very much in love. Nailed the whole thing.'

'So what happened with Sonja?'

'I knew what she was doing. Where I come from, everyone talks. She'd say she was out with work friends and my friends would see her with another man. Always white guys, too. Like she had to try something off-menu.'

I giggled. 'That's the first time I've ever heard of a white person being referred to as exotic.'

'You grow up like Sonja and I did, where your entire family and social life is geared around your community, they kind of are. All my exes looked and talked like her. All her exes could have been me.'

'Sounds to me like arranged marriage by design.'

'You're not wrong,' Himesh said, searching for somewhere to dispose of his cigarette before crushing it beneath his battered Gazelles.

I reached down to scoop up Lola, who was coming dangerously close to eating the smouldering butts for tea. She purred in agreement when she saw Himesh, displaying the unbelievable level of familiarity that she also seemed to have with every tenant in the building. What a total floozy of an animal.

'Let me get this straight. You caught her in flagrante with Jonathan the investment banker and threw her out onto the street.'

'That would have made for a better story but no, it was nothing as cinematic as that. She uploaded a very racy photo that was clearly meant for a private DM to her profile by mistake. So I finally figured out what she was up to for sure at almost exactly the same time as all my mates and every one of my cousins in this time zone.'

'Oh Himesh,' I said, sadly. 'That is so fucked.'

'Look, I've had better Friday nights.'

'How do you ever come back from something like that?'

'In the first instance, you don't. You make that split-second calculation, which in my case was to pack a weekend bag, disappear to my friend's place in Fulham, smoke copious amounts of weed, listen to FKA Twigs and not answer my phone to anyone; not her, not my sister, not my dad, nobody, for two weeks.'

'What was the plan?'

'Oblivion, basically. I didn't have a framework beyond that. I'm betting that's around where you are now.'

'Sort of. Except I didn't piss off anywhere. This is my place.'

'But you said you made the decision. So it doesn't really matter who is physically still here. Sonja didn't leave our flat. When I came back, I think it was nearly three months later, it was as I'd left it.'

'Like a time capsule.'

'Sort of.'

'He's been gone four months.'

'There's no statute of limitations in this country. You're in it; it'll take as long as it takes.'

'Unless I end it.'

'This is what I've been trying to tell you for the last half hour. You've already ended it. But you haven't finished it. They're different states. I ended things with Sonja. I just decided one day that I wasn't ready for our story to really be over. I missed her so much it felt like food poisoning. I couldn't keep anything else down.'

'Still, that's a remarkable turnaround. If I were you, I'd set Lola on her to scratch her bleeding eyes out.'

'Oh I definitely entertained all those thoughts.' He laughed. 'What else is there to do when you're high and watching *Peep Show* for the tenth time?'

'You definitely strike me as a Jez, you know.'

'Did you hear the part where I told you I had twin girls? Is that a Jez thing to do?'

'No, but going back to a woman who treats you like shit . . . actually, that's more of a Mark vibe, isn't it.'

'I assume you get Big Suze a lot.'

'Because of my height or my undeniable good looks?'

'No,' he said, suddenly serious. 'Because you've spent most of your life as someone else's love interest.'

It was getting too cold to hang about outside much longer. I ushered Himesh, this man who had come to make a simple purchase nearly three hours ago, back in through the double doors and into the flat. Lola leapt from my arms and darted in ahead of us before I could stop her. Her owners, wherever they were, were in for another sleepless night.

'Right then; it's £1800 for the table, and if you'd be so kind as to relieve me of the chairs, I'll do the lot for £2000.'

Himesh scrunched up his face in thought.

'That's . . . wait a second, didn't the ad say £2500?'

'Thought I'd try my luck, but you just can't put a price on such a wonderful evening talking ethics with a dashing young dad.'

'Listen, I can't take it from you. It's not right.'

'Really, Himesh? Come on.'

He walked over to the fridge and pulled it open. My single pot of yoghurt, half-empty jar of gherkins and overripe punnet of blueberries looked even more grim when viewed through the eyes of a stranger.

'For starters, I think you could probably use that extra dosh.'

'I hate to be that person, but you need to know that romcoms lie,' I said, leaning past him to slam the fridge door shut. 'Sad single women don't eat ice cream by the tub, wailing along to Adele until one day we miraculously feel better. We starve ourselves. Half a meal, twice a day, supported by supplements that are mostly placebos until eventually we look so fit that someone half-decent wants to take us to bed again. It's a ritual as old as England herself.'

'Oh, my mistake. So this is the fridge of a healthy person.'

'A healthy person would probably leave out the blueberries. Too much sugar.'

Seeing as Himesh had already crossed the line, it was nice to know I could step back over it myself. He rolled his eyes and, raising his hands in mock resignation, moved back towards the table, which he tried, pointlessly, to lift himself. Even his grunt was unconvincing.

'Money and diets aside, this thing weighs a ton,' he said.

'A hundred kilos. Again, very clearly stated on the listing. Did you smoke so much weed you forgot how to read?'

'It's a family table. Your family table.'

'I'm nearly thirty-seven and single. Right now, I eat most of my meals out of a pot or over the sink. How do you fancy my chances?'

'Chance is what it's all about,' Himesh interjected. 'The chance he comes back. The chance you make up. The chance that one day, you have a family of your own and you have to source some shite table from *MADE* because a few years ago, you offloaded this one to me.'

'If you're so fucking confident, let's make a deal,' I snapped, smacking my hand down on the table. 'Should any or all of those totally unfathomable events transpire, I have your number. I'll give you a bell and you can just bring it right back to help complete my perfect life in my perfect home.'

Himesh bent over to pick up his canvas bag, slinging it over his shoulder. I wondered if this was the same one he'd lived out of for a few months after he'd pulled his own disappearing act. It seemed roomy enough.

'You said you'd tell me if I was overstepping.'

'I'm sorry, it wasn't clear to you?'

'I always try to mend things. It's a problem I have. Sonja and I discussed it in therapy; I get over-invested in fixing things that don't need to be fixed.'

'Or can't.'

'Or can't.'

*Sold the bloody thing,* I texted Oli, who was definitely watching some loud film on his projector next door and wouldn't hear me knock. *Can I borrow ur big guns for 10 mins plssssss. Promise last time x*

'All I know is if I can make someone else's existence a tiny bit better while mine circles the drain, the universe will repay me with kindness.'

'Ah,' Himesh smiled wryly, 'a champagne Buddhist.'

Like clockwork, there was a rap at the door.

'Price just went back up,' I said. 'Last chance.'

'I can't say no to an offer that bad,' he replied, rummaging through his bag for his car keys. 'I'm going to call you in six months. If he's back, I'm bringing it back.'

'Do I get to keep the money?'

'It's a return, not a refund. Yes, you do.'

'This is Himesh,' I said to Oli, who'd quietly let himself in with our spare key. 'He's relatively insane but mostly harmless.'

'Sounds like my kind of chap,' Oli chuckled, sizing up the table and realising the enormity of the task he'd so selflessly agreed to help me out with.

'Now tell me,' he said, rolling up the sleeves of his flannel. 'How did you even get this fucker in here?'

# INTERMEZZI: FOXES

Before moving to London, Elly had never seen a fox in the wild. And before she and Enzo had settled in at Academy Apartments, she'd never heard foxes have sex.

The sound still haunts her regularly; a grating, yelpy shriek whose closest parallel is that of a newborn baby crying out in pain. Even after many years in the flat, during which she has grown accustomed to the assorted nocturnal rumblings of Pembury circus – the jungle sirens of 2 am ambulances tearing past, the throbbing hum of the Five Points Brewery secretly dispatching kegs after hours and the inevitable tambourine jingle that signals the return of the local rudeboys, intent on their quest to scale the security fence and make off with all the bikes in the courtyard – it is the foxes alone that yank her out of sleep by the scruff of her neck. They seem to be closer to her window each time.

Elly is not someone who spooks easily, but after Enzo left, maybe on the second or third night, when she thought she might manage to get a few decent hours' kip, she dug her heels in and dragged their queen bed, base and all, to the other side of the room, as far from the window as possible. Thanks to the former school's questionable architecture, this side slopes upward, and Elly's head nearly glances the ceiling each time she buries herself beneath the covers. But she prefers it this way. Enzo is a small man, but in his absence, their room has become cavernous, never-ending. Elly bunches the duvet and pillows around her torso, coiling them tighter and tighter and willing her body to become more compact, so that she might be lucky and wake up feeling like someone is holding her.

She has resisted the temptation to go full Bridget Jones, resuming smoking and enjoying it, but never in bed – at least not yet. Similarly, Elly feels her gin to water ratio is appropriate given the seismic events of the past months. Besides, there's nobody here to argue the point; she has been alone in this place for ages.

But she has taken to blaring PJ Harvey and Nilüfer Yanya at almost deafening decibel levels, free at last from the soulless, genericised house music that has been permeating the very fabric of London like a disease, bleating out from tinny off-licence speakers and souped-up Uber radios; flat, one-dimensional shite that spins hooks from the '90s in a warped simulacrum for kids who aren't old enough to know the reference points, something she is convinced feels deliberately emotionless. As her own form of rebellion, Elly pumps Polly Jean deep into the night, re-reading her old journals while vacantly streaming porn she isn't even into and eventually passing out with the lights on, anonymous bodies still grinding onscreen, which naturally attracts the foxes.

The foxes fuck like it's their last night on Earth. They swoon and howl, wounded and satiated all at once – clearly PJ's spirit animals, Elly thinks, as their frenzied scurrying pulls her back into undesired consciousness. She knows from hard-won experience that the foxes are not the wham-bam type; they will tussle and bite and claw and yap for up to ninety minutes at a time. Elly groans and rolls over to her bedside table, where her most recent journal sits under an unfinished drink, scattered painkillers and a completely futile bag of earplugs.

Over the past few evenings, Elly has been trying to get down on paper what it is that she finds so fascinating about these foxes that fuck. She has been wrestling with the notion that they represent something irrevocably true about modern relationships, with their double helix of pleasure and pain. But Elly has always been more of a sketcher than a word-wrangler. Unless it's stream-of-consciousness, that flow state she can only achieve after the precise combination of a good yoga session, strong coffee and most of her colleagues being out of the office on a pitch, metaphors tend not to come easily to her. Beyond the now-far window, the foxes reach the first of a likely five codas to their lovemaking. The raw violence of it all still thrills Elly. At the same time, on her discarded laptop screen, an unknown woman works two penises at once. She is rubbing furiously and methodically, and as the foxes reach climax, the anonymous members inside the browser window spray the woman in the face and she is dead-eyed as she smiles, holding the two spent organs in her hands as if to say, 'Is this all there is?'

And as Elly reaches over to shut the MacBook before her battery depletes itself, the digital moaning and analogue yowling competing with the omnipresent, groggy whine inside her skull, the correct phrasing finally arrives in her brain and she quickly hunches over the black Moleskine, scribbling wildly.

The foxes are not just pleasure and pain.
They are pleasure *as* pain, or maybe more usefully,
*pain as pleasure.*
When foxes fuck it's both these states at once.
They aren't trying to separate good times from bad,
nice experiences from not-nice ones.
Foxes understand – biologically? – that to trust
someone as your mate, as your partner, is to accept
that even when they love you, they will hurt you.
(Or that you will do the same to them.)
We spend our lives in artificially constructed
relationships, trying to maximise positivity, then
feeling pain when our mate leaves or abandons us.
Humans should learn from foxes and fuck like it
could damage us at any minute.
We should dig in our claws and love in a way that
causes other people alarm.
Otherwise it's just performance.

Foxes get that. Foxes are smarter than us.

Elly turns out the light and falls into the deepest sleep she's had in a very long time. She wakes up so disastrously late for work that she decides if anyone asks, she'll say she's taking one of those new mental health 'duvet days' they keep banging on about.

Luckily for her, the entire team is out on a pitch.

Nobody even notices she isn't there.

# IV. DVD BOX SET

Shoreditch House was full of wankers, almost from the outset. But it had also been designed by Tom Dixon, something of a god to people like Elly. As with most of Nick Jones' creations, wanker demand soon outstripped supply, and queues for the lifts, which snaked around the lavish Cowshed gift shop by the ground floor entrance and deep into Ebor Street, could take hours. Sensing inevitability, one of Elly's two bosses had made a habit of ending Fridays at precisely 3.30 pm, so that by 4 at the latest, she'd be double-parked with two overpriced cocktails on an eye-wateringly beautiful leather armchair while pretending she enjoyed socialising.

As an olive branch to the firm's employees, none of whom were particularly well paid, the partners quickly signed them up for early memberships, which were covered as long as they stayed with the company. This made logical sense as the middle two floors were beautifully laid out and the perfect place to pitch to new clients, while the door was managed so fastidiously that despite the hype around the venue, none of the three bars were ever overly full. Elly's office was but a six-minute walk away from Shoreditch House, and much to her private despair, it became a walk she did regularly.

She'd brought Enzo along a few times. They'd been together nearly five years by then and it seemed only fair for him to understand the sort of extracurricular pressures she had to undergo after work hours. She should have known better; networking was Enzo's blood type. He charmed the pants off everyone, listened and responded with genuine curiosity and always seemed to manage to have an Aperol in his hands without having paid for it. Sure, you'd never catch him dead in a black T-shirt and jeans, the unofficial uniform of Elly's co-workers, but Enzo's fish-out-of-water status didn't seem to faze him in the slightest. Striding into packed rooms full of insecure, public-school graduates with charge accounts was something he had been unofficially training for his entire life. Besides, Enzo frequently profiled colourful individuals with staggering net worth for his day job. Shoreditch House was a regular playground for him.

Elly soon realised that if she kept inviting her partner, she'd never get a word in, and as much as she hated vacuous conversation, post-work boozing was a relatively pain-free and well-trodden road to a pay rise. By 2013, she'd been to Shoreditch House so many times that she could recite its gym and yoga schedules by heart. Elly knew every receptionist and

DJ by name, she could tell you which levels had the better vodka, and she'd located the labyrinthine rooms hidden behind dummy bookcases, where one could either discreetly snort blow or blow someone. Despite this intimate level of knowledge, she mostly watched the comings and goings of the place with the air of a detached observer, rarely engaging in conversation and never expecting anything genuinely interesting to happen.

Without labouring the point, her chance encounter with Michael was definitely not on Elly's bingo card for the late summer of 2013.

'So does nobody know how to treat a lady in this city or are all these guys just total pussies in expensive sneakers?'

The guy looked familiar, the way all vaguely famous Americans look vaguely familiar: big teeth, great hair and dramatically smaller than expected, almost a scale model of how they appeared on screen. He had searching eyes that shifted subtly between green and brown, which framed a Roman nose you could build a moat around. He struck Elly as the kind of man who frequently got what he wanted, and even though she couldn't place him just yet, she felt the sudden, illicit rush of wanting to be someone he wanted.

The cool edge to the evening signalled the imminent foreclosure of the high season. She had been sitting by the pool and smoking, mainly because it still seemed novel to her that it was allowed up here, but also because it afforded her a whole floor's distance from her co-workers, most of whom were currently occupying the same gender-neutral bathroom stall. Her tall glass was almost empty. Between drags, she sucked absent-mindedly on melting ice cubes.

He flopped down on the recliner next to her and sighed like he'd never seen a pool lit up at night before.

'You got a light?'

'I don't smoke,' she said.

'Me neither. But somehow, we both got cigarettes in our mitts.'

Elly waved at a guy with a formidable septum piercing a few seats over, who duly lobbed his tiny purple Bic back in her direction.

The man took a long puff and stared out at the skyline of former factories turned apartments.

'We have one of these places in New York, you know, but I've never been.'

'Istanbul next,' she replied. 'The creative class has metastasised.'

'Yeah, I don't get that whole membership thing. Seems very English. You guys love a class system, don't you?'

She took the last sip of her gin and thought about it.

'I suppose you could say it's a hangover from colonialism. We have fewer countries to lord it over these days, but we'll always have each other.'

'I thought the whole vibe here was meant to be about being a writer or an artist or a filmmaker or some shit,' he said, magicking another Marlboro from his jacket pocket and offering it to her before relighting his own. 'But all I see are rich pricks.'

Elly laughed. 'Who else can afford to be an artist?'

'So what's your deal?' he said, eyes still stuck on her.

'Oh, I'm far worse than all of these people,' she said, lowering her voice as if revealing a devastating secret. 'I'm . . . a designer.'

The man cracked up, breaking the intensity with which he'd been staring at her for the last ten minutes.

'That's fuckin' hilarious. What do you design, birthday cards?'

'Buildings, mostly. The insides of them, like this one.'

'And people pay you for that? To pick wallpaper and choose chairs?'

'Quite handsomely. Well, my firm, anyway. I get paid just enough to bum fags from other creative types.'

'You English with your slang,' he chuckled. 'If you talked like that where I'm from, you'd be dead meat.'

Blood Orange's *Cupid Deluxe* had started filtering through the outdoor speakers, as it would across London rooftops that season. The sounds of South African marimba, mournful jazz saxophone and Nile Rodgers–style guitar chords rang out across the deck; Dev Hynes' most successful reincarnation yet. It could just as easily have been 1983 as 2013, this ganache of upwardly mobile flesh set over private parties in New York, or Tokyo, or Berlin. Perhaps this was the ultimate end game of the Soho House project, Elly thought to herself, already at the precipice of being too wasted to form logical thoughts. Standardising expensive monoculture.

Septum and his lithe Ghanaian friend had made the executive decision to go swimming, likely spurred on by whatever was in the flask they'd been topping their drinks up with all night. They paddled over to where Elly was sitting, searching for their lilac lighter.

'Holy shit,' Septum said, tattoos glowing under the pool's lights. 'You're not . . .'

'No,' the guy said abruptly. 'Don't worry. I get it all the time.'

'I mean, you just look so much like him.'

'Lots of people look like lots of people,' the guy said. 'It don't mean shit.'

Elly blinked through the smoke and the gins and overly heaped bump she'd snorted in the disabled bathroom just after she'd texted Enzo to say she was on her way home. It amazed her that she hadn't seen it earlier. Who else could it possibly be? His hair had seriously greyed, but it had been at least a decade, right? She even knew his real name, not his character's, which might have endeared her more to him if she'd said it instead of blurting out –

'You're Chrissy. Chrissy Moltisanti.'

Elly loved telly as much as the next person, but what was now breathlessly referred to as the 'golden age' of prestige programming had mostly passed her by. To be fair, multi-series character arcs and frequent, feature-length episodes didn't exactly gel that well with the lifestyle of a young Londoner. One didn't even have to be a particularly social thirty-something to still find themselves out of the house three to four nights per week, which left little time to commit to hour-long instalments devoted to James Gandolfini's slowly unravelling psyche. A year or so before meeting Enzo, Elly had briefly dated an American – disappointingly named Brad – who had spent many an evening trying to impress upon her the vital importance of *The Wire*. Brad's earnestness, along with his fixation on chewing gum both before and after every meal, had become intensely grating and turned Elly off the notion of ever binging the equivalent of four full days of her life on some TV show, no matter how many awards it had won.

As with most stories she told Enzo about her suboptimal romantic past, he failed to see the root of the problem, focusing instead on a chance for betterment. The looming *Sopranos* box set arrived under the Christmas tree they'd wrangled from Columbia Flower Market, looking more like a task than a gift and proving that even the most stand-up men still only ever hear what they want to hear.

'Eighty-six hours!' Elly whistled, inspecting the back cover. 'Is this a present or a prison sentence?'

*The Sopranos* had not received the same rapturous response in Italy as it had in the US, and due to its violent content, it was relegated to a late-night slot on Canale 5 that only bored teenagers like Enzo had stayed up to watch. He'd seen the majority of *I Soprano* when he was still far too young to understand it, with Tony dubbed by Stefano De Santo, a famous voice artist who also frequently transliterated Robert De Niro. Enzo's move to the UK coincided with the show's penultimate season and he watched the finale with his housemates in English, which had proven deeply unsatisfying. In Elly, he saw the chance to start over and relive the entire story as intended. He'd also correctly predicted that they were in for a shockingly brutal winter, for which couch snuggles, TV and takeout were the only acceptable solution.

Despite her initial reluctance, between Christmas and New Year, Elly and Enzo watched *The Sopranos* in full – twice. They had long-ranging discussions over dinner, in bed and via text about Paulie keeping the painting of Tony on the horse, whether Carmela should have upped and left with Furio and how Adriana might have gotten out of it all alive. Elly found herself reading the additional liner notes over breakfast. She fossicked through IMDb while on the bus. She couldn't remember being as preoccupied with anything since forcing her pa to take her to see Take That at the G-Mex when she was eleven. And then, just as quickly as she'd ditched Robbie for Scary and Sporty, the seasons changed, the snow melted, and she and Enzo emerged from their flat, forgetting all about New Jersey's favourite crime family. That is, until one of them appeared in front of her in the flesh.

Like the Soho Houses in Dean and Greek Street from which it took its nomenclature, Shoreditch House had a strict no photography rule, and in essence, that's where the rules ended. Guarded by exclusivity and unwatched by increasingly sophisticated camera phones, the denizens of Jones' latest inner-city playground could get away with almost anything short of murder.

So when Elly told her two most trusted girlfriends over recovery pints at The Pembury that she'd met Michael Imperioli by the pool on the roof, and that she'd momentarily considered having it off with him but decided against it, they had to take her word for it. Whether it really happened or didn't, and even if she'd imagined him entirely, his strong hand on her back while they talked, her long feet with chipped nail polish dangling in the water yet somehow not even cold, there was no concrete proof. It was also mostly beside the point; that she entertained the notion at all pointed to something subtle coming apart in her relationship, a certain intransigence on her part to become a wife and mother, to step into the role that was so obviously on the cards for women in her romantic position. To stay in most nights, put the little ones to bed and watch *Bake Off* until her eyes glazed over, every day another ring in the daisy chain of mundanity. Upon hearing this theory, her friends seemed suspect. If he really was just a manifestation, Lucy said as she headed to the bar for more crisps, would you still be madly going on about it?

But it cannot be an accident, Elly thought as she rode Roxy past fading trees in Vicky Park to clear her fogged-up brain, that last winter Enzo bought her a box set of *The Sopranos* and less than a year later, she could have drunkenly shagged its deuteragonist.

Of course, there were cameras in Shoreditch House. Don't be daft. With a fit-out that costly, it would be foolish not to have them installed all over the building, cleverly camouflaged behind the dark wood panelling. On the third floor, in a small, well-lit room behind the gym that not even Elly knew about, two round-the-clock security guards sat in fancy office chairs monitoring the movements of the liberated creative class across every square inch of the building – even the supposedly private ones. As with all staff in the Soho House group, these guards were encouraged to remain inconspicuous. They were to look and dress and talk like any other house member. One of them wore Lanvin trousers and a rare New Balance colourway that cost 600 quid on resale. He played absent-mindedly with a small, purple lighter. His colleague, freshly showered, was fully inked with delicate linework, but memorable mostly for his large septum piercing.

Understandably fascinated by this chance meeting of celebrity and civilian, they had eyes on Elly and Michael all night. And it really was all night; when Amadou and Jess knocked quietly to relieve them at 6 am, the pair in question were still by the pool, barely moving but still talking, completely oblivious to what time it was. Septum blinked, his eyes like plaster. He hadn't moved from this screen since he got back from the roof five hours ago.

'That's Chrissy,' he told Amadou. 'From *The Sopranos*.'

'Get out.'

'They've been going since the afternoon – yesterday,' he said. 'Josef and I have a hundred-pound wager on what happens next.'

'You guys get paid too much,' Jess laughed, grabbing a spare chair and wheeling over to take a closer look.

'Don't we close in an hour?'

'Half six we throw the stragglers out,' said Josef. 'That gives my man here twenty minutes to find a cash point.'

Septum grinned. 'You are sorely mistaken. They are 100 per cent going home together.'

'I don't know,' Amadou said. 'Would they not have done it already? What's she waiting for?'

'Exactly my point,' said Josef. 'He's got to be at least twenty years older than her. He's not going to want her to see him in the cold light of day.'

'You know, I've never seen *The Sopranos*,' Jess said. 'My ex was obsessed with it so I made a vow never to watch it. Useless prick.'

'You are missing out, doll,' Septum said, still not taking his eyes off the top left screen, where suddenly he noticed signs of movement.

'Yes yes yes, here we go!'

The four crowded in around the monitor.

Elly was drunk enough not to know exactly what was happening, but not so far gone that she didn't realise the light in her eyes was the beginning of the sun coming up. She hiccupped loudly, uncontrollably. It felt like she had been hiccupping her entire life. Her breath was laced with so much gin she may well have been flammable. There was a man she didn't really know holding his hand out to her, helping her up out of the chair. She held him for balance, trying to pull her double vision back into one.

*

In the now-stuffy security room, Septum clapped his hands together animatedly.

'This is it. Just transfer me now, Josef, I beg, save the effort and the heartbreak.'

'Listen, big man. If I don't see no bum grabbing or snogging before they walk out those doors, you're not getting so much as a Rizla out of me.'

'Will you shut up, both of you?' Jess said. 'Something's happening.'

'Just tell me, did anything happen?' Elly burps.

'What, like did we fuck? Honey, we've been up here for like twelve whole hours. I don't know how you guys do it over here, but I usually like to get naked when there aren't hundreds of people around.'

'Okay, fab. Good. Great.'

'Well, glad I could make your day,' Michael said.

'No, it's not like that, it's just I . . .'

'You have a boyfriend. I know. Italian guy. Serious. You've been talking about him nonstop.'

'I have?'

She totters by the edge of the pool and he grabs her by the waist to keep her upright.

'I've had a really great time hanging out with you,' he said, pulling back and staring her in the face, just like he did when they first met. 'And you have an honest-to-god next level ass. But you really need to go home.'

Elly watched as a new day flooded over the misaligned Shoreditch horizon. She wondered if Enzo was still awake, or if he was even still in the flat at all. Perhaps he'd intuited what she'd been up to and booked himself on the next EasyJet flight back home to Naples, crushed heart carefully stowed in his carry-on.

She spun back around.

'Hold on, what did you say about my bum?'

But Chrissy was already gone.

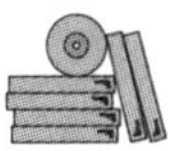

**Jane Rawson 23.32**

**Hi, is this still available?**

It had taken Jane some time to thoroughly convince me that she was a real person. Of course it bloody well had. For a start, she didn't seem to know how to use the internet at all. She wrote in full sentences with perfect grammar and it took her about twenty-five minutes to compose a single response. I could just imagine her, bent over some ancient PC with one of those clickety-clack keyboards, punching out each letter slowly with her index fingers. The woman kept me up until midnight having a conversation that in real life might have taken three minutes. It was excruciating.

07.20

I have to tell you, Eloise, this is most exciting. I can't believe you have the entire set, with the bonus discs too! It is Eloise, isn't it? I hope I haven't made an erroneous assumption.

07.22

yep. only mum calls me that tho

08.15

I can't imagine why not, it's a beautiful name. I believe the etymology is French but it's been adapted all over the world. My girls are called Rosalind and Ophelia. (I have a thing for The Bard 😛

08.17

& tony soprano apparently.

10.05

You've no idea. I don't really know how to use Facebook, but Ros told me at dinner the other evening that there was someone selling *The Sopranos* – the whole set, no less – so I made her sign me up at once just so I could speak to you.

10.22

well, here we are. so you wanna pick it up from me or I can meet you somewhere central if it's easier

10.51

I'd feel rather uncomfortable entering a stranger's house for a transaction.

10.51
you should tell that to everyone else i've sold shit to lately.

11.30
If it isn't a huge bother, there's a little place in Soho where I like to while away the evening hours after work. We could have a drink or two and talk about *The Sopranos*. Or maybe you could tell me your story? My daughter mentioned you seem to be selling off your entire life. If that's not too forward.

11.45
sounds good. also, did you mean to use that emoji?

Persuaded by Jane's passionate pursuit of the box set and spurred on, honestly, by near-toxic levels of boredom, we exchanged numbers and the next Wednesday I found myself in a small cocktail bar off Old Compton Street that I'd somehow never been inside despite hearing about it dozens of times from Enzo, carting that bloated, 27-disc collection in a reusable plastic Sainsbury's bag like some sort of mad woman.

I honestly hadn't expected to sell *The Sopranos* at all. Streaming had arrived in England over the winter and it was painfully clear to me and everyone I knew that the DVD – much like its predecessors – was about to become extinct. Unlike vinyl, it was far too soon for the format to revive itself as a cultural artefact, especially while it was still in a protracted state of dying. There was a digital lag before you were catapulted face-first into the next version of the future, and that was the precise window I found myself in as I arrived at the bar. Nobody was disputing that *The Sopranos* had firmly cemented its place in the canon, but equally, investing in something you'd soon have no means of watching seemed like a remarkably foolish idea. It was like buying a rare CD, only to remember neither your car nor computer could play them anymore.

I didn't tell Jane any of this, as I was disastrously behind on rent. Lex's deal had seemed too good to be true – and it was, assuming you had a partner with whom to divide it. Alone, I was . . . well, I was eating olives for supper again. And not the fancy Spanish ones from M&S, either. I'd found being relatively destitute suited my state of mind, but being hungry by choice was still quite different from having to move out to E12 or worse, back home with my parents in Manchester.

'Coffee after six! You must be European.'

'No, I was just married to one.'

'Oh goody. Then we have lots to talk about.'

Jane had lovely blue-green eyes and shoulder-length grey hair so perfectly tinted it seemed like it had always been her natural colour. Within five minutes of meeting her, during which I'd ordered a macchiato to silence the insistent screaming of my Current Account Balance and she'd corrected my mistake by summoning the waiter and requesting two house-style negronis instead, she had already struck me as the type of rare older person who had never given up on feeling young. Jane cackled with wicked abandon when she laughed, revealing a backline of gold and silver crowns. She leaned in close and listened actively. It would only strike me much later, as I haphazardly walked home, that despite being some twenty years younger, she reminded me a lot of my pa.

'My ex-husband and I used to live not far from here, in Fitzrovia. He didn't care much for Soho, especially during the nineties. "Filth and fags, that's all there is down there," Gregory liked to say.'

'Charming,' I said.

'Well, that's the problem. He really was. An absolute beast behind closed doors, mind you, especially after we had our children, but put him in any room anywhere in the city and every other person would leave with those big cartoon love hearts in their eyes.'

'Except around here, I take it.'

'Oh, he went to all the members' clubs – especially those gentlemen's ones where they got up to all sorts of nonsense while we were home raising the children. But I wouldn't say he was a devotee of the area, no. He'd sooner ramble the streets of Paris than Central London, my Gregory.'

'How did you end up finding this place, then? It's quite, er . . . niche.'

Jane gulped down the last of her negroni, which I had an inkling would not be her final drink of the evening.

'I suppose what happens is you have kids and you leave your job because your husband is rich – preposterously rich, really – and then one morning you wake up and your two daughters are teenage girls and they don't need you to mother them anymore, so you wander the streets and you spend too much time and money in Foyles and you show up here in their first week of opening and you never really leave.'

'My husb– ex-husband, I think it was the same for him,' I said. 'I still remember the day he came home after discovering this place, whooping and hollering about how *autentico* it was. He was honestly like a pig in shit.'

Jane smirked. 'Was he in the cocktail or espresso set? I may have run into him, you know . . .'

'I think you'd remember,' I sighed. 'Very handsome, very animated and very short.'

'I'll conduct a search of the ancient vault,' she said, tapping the side of her head. 'How recent?'

'How recently was he here?'

'You corrected yourself before. When you started talking about him. One assumes he's only recently taken on the mantle of "ex-husband".'

'Jane! I thought I was here to drop you some DVDs, not face a jury trial. Besides, it's just something I say to help me deal with it. We're not properly divorced yet.'

'I understand,' she said. 'But it seems like you have nothing but sorrow at the moment. And I have nothing but time.'

*

There were four styles of negroni on Termini's limited menu and Jane insisted I try them all.

'Don't worry about the bill,' she said. 'Consider it karmic retribution for all those times he never brought you here.'

'I don't blame him, really. We all need our own private universes.'

'Something that's just for us,' Jane said.

'Exactly.'

'I think I've seen *The Sopranos* at least six or seven times, start to finish,' she continued. 'It came out around the time Ofie was born and I recall it was a horrible winter. Gregory was away in Switzerland, bailing out some billionaire for not paying his inheritance tax and I was stuck at home with this crippling postpartum depression. It was brutally cold, the draught got through all the windows. Ros was teething and screaming the house down and this new one, she wouldn't bloody latch, she ripped my poor tits to shreds and we had all this help, obviously, but hired help doesn't fix your mind. When you're down there, in that well, you really need your loved ones to pull you out. Gregory would fly in every few weeks, and I would mooch around the house like I was already dead. I wanted to be dead. Lord, I did. I hated myself; I hated the life I was trapped in and I hated how much I hated my kids.'

'That sounds . . . horrendous.'

'Truly. And the thing that happens when you're blue for that long, which none of the books tell you – and I was an English teacher before I married up, so I've read them all – is that it doesn't make you brittle. It turns you hard. You freeze into ice. Nothing can get through, but you keep searching for something, anything that will. So one night, when we'd finally managed to put Ros down and I'd figured out how to get Ophelia to feed for more than two minutes, I was sitting in our lounge, flicking through the ten million cable channels my husband paid for but was never home long enough to watch and I see this man, this giant, hulking Jersey Potato of a man, standing out the back of his house and having some epiphany about ducks, right before he drives into town and beats some guy to death. I can't tell you; it was like someone had opened me up at the back and put in a fresh set of batteries.'

'It's an incredible show,' I offered. 'I used to say to my husband that it was closer to a piece of art.'

'Absolutely,' Jane said, bouncing forward on her patent leather seat. 'As soon as it finished, I started watching re-runs. I think it saved my life.'

'Did you ever watch it with Gregory?'

'No.' She chuckled mirthlessly. 'I think he lasted half an episode. He really didn't like Carmela because she was so mouthy. Found it all quite base, you know. So I had it all to myself. My own private universe.'

I rummaged around in the bag beneath my feet, fishing out the chunky box set and placing it on the small table between us.

'But . . . you never bought it?'

'I never had to. It was always available. But then I left Gregory and I left that set-top box, too. And yes, I know all about this new Netflix thing, but as I'm sure you know, this is an HBO program, and they don't have those on Netflix yet.

One day it'll be there, I'm sure, but I've already lost it once. I want to have it with me now, no matter what happens.'

'What happened to Gregory?' I asked.

'Oh,' she said, wiping her eyes, 'I left him. It took far too long, but I left him. Gregory was very traditional, very blue-blooded. Could trace his lineage directly back to the nobility in the 1300s or something ridiculous. His family name was extremely important to him.'

'And you had two daughters.'

'It was never going to be enough for him. Two healthy, intelligent girls who could do anything and all he wanted was a son. I couldn't do it. My body couldn't do it. I tried to reason with him, but honestly, it was like trying to reason with Tony Soprano. Men like that, winning is in their blood. They'll flip entire worlds upside down just to get their own way.'

Jane paused to swirl the remaining ice in her drink.

'We lived in a large townhouse, but the rows we used to have, you could hear us from the street.'

'Were you scared?'

'I was, but I wasn't. I grew up on an estate in Homerton and my mother died when I was fifteen. Having nothing didn't terrify me, really; nothing is where I came from. Gregory and I only crossed paths because his brother was the headmaster of the school I taught at. He invited me over to his family's place for Christmas. It's all up to the gods, really. Everything in life.'

'I take it you don't live in Fitzrovia anymore,' I said.

'No, dear. I am back east, with a very kind man called Nicholas. He never shouts at me.'

I laughed. 'I live in Hackney; we're practically neighbours. Why on Earth are we all the way over here on a school night?'

Jane smiled sadly. 'When I can't spend time with Tony, Chrissy and Paulie,' she said, 'it comforts me to be around real Italians.'

The bar, I eventually realised, was set up to look like the interior of the dining carriage of a train, the kind they did exceptionally well on national rail services from Switzerland and Italy but that in the UK typically just became places for parents to secretly drink away from their children. There couldn't have been room for more than twenty-five people in total, yet Termini swelled with a kind of infectious joie de vivre that spilled into the street, where those still waiting for a booth chattered loudly while nursing takeaway aperitifs.

Sitting and watching the carnival around me, where everyone seemed to know the staff, stashing their coats in the faux-luggage racks above our heads and signalling for another round, felt like being the centre of the universe. It was no wonder Enzo loved it here; it was the sort of intoxicating place that made you feel like you never had anywhere else to be.

Also, I was intoxicated.

'I haven't dined out on this story in a while,' I slurred, 'but I feel like you of all people will appreciate it.'

I'd been drinking pretty regularly since Enzo and I had split, but I was clearly no match for Jane, who steamed through cocktails like they were orange Lucozade. Had I been less inebriated, I might have felt almost humbled by this fact.

Jane leaned in, sensing my swimminess. 'If you don't mind, I'll order us some prosciutto and burrata first. I'm practically 100 per cent Campari at this point.'

'G-good idea,' I burped. 'But please, let me pay for some of this.'

'Darling,' Jane tut-tutted. 'Your company is worth far more to me than a few slices of shaved swine.'

As was always the way, I didn't appreciate precisely how drunk I was until I started eating. I'd clocked up at least ninety minutes with Jane, which I felt afforded me the licence to throw all my social graces out the window, so I heaped cheese onto my plate, telling my one famous tale while also shovelling cured pig into my mouth. It occurred to me, as I chewed loudly and undignifiedly, that I hadn't eaten properly in some time.

'Christopher,' I finally managed to get out between stringy chews.

'Tony's nephew?'

'The same.'

'Such an amazingly well-rounded character,' Jane said. 'Do you know he also wrote a few of the episodes?'

'Someone told me that once.'

'He plays a failed screenwriter when really, he was quite successful at it. Something about that tickles me.'

'He was my favourite too,' I said. 'Him and Paulie. I thought Paulie was ridiculous but also very endearing as a person. There was something so beautifully sad about him, you know? In that vest, just sitting alone in front of the TV, waiting for Tony to come over. But Christopher, he was always more nuanced to me.'

'And quite sexy, in a way,' Jane said, fishing prosciutto fat from behind her molars. 'Pig that he was. Him and Adriana, hoo-oooh! I remember sitting alone in the big house, watching the two of them go for it and thinking, "I want a man to want me like that."'

'Jane,' I laughed, 'can I tell the bloody story?'

'Oh yes, please do! I'm just, very . . . excitable when I drink.'

'That's okay. In a way, what you've told me makes the story better, anyway, because . . . er . . .'

'Out with it, woman! You what?'

'I . . . I think I may have shagged him.'

'Who?'

'Christopher. Well, Michael, the guy who plays him, anyway.'

Something about the braggadocio associated with the story, the way it immediately changed me in the eyes of whomever I shared it with, always made me feel awkward. I stared at the floor.

It took Jane a minute to gather herself.

'Well,' she said finally. 'I'm not sure I can top that.'

'I'm not proud of it. I was in a long-term relationship. He was about to propose to me.'

'The ex? Very handsome, very short?'

'That's the one.'

'My dear, it seems as though you have a type.'

'Don't.' I giggled. 'Don't you start.'

'Alright, Deliverer of The Sopranos Who Has Also Gone To Bed With *An Actual Character*. I require some supporting evidence.'

'You know the Soho House around the corner, on Greek Street? They opened one in Shoreditch a few years ago.'

'Yes, I've heard of it. Ofie's work has parties there sometimes. Pool on the roof, yes? *Very* East London working class . . .'

'Believe me, I hate it there. But my bosses adore it, and our office is around the corner.'

'So, you met him there?'

'I should preface this by saying I was plastered. At least, I was by the time I left the next morning. I think I went to bed for the next two days.'

'I'm trying to visualise how this happens,' Jane said.

'Well, I'm sitting by the pool and I'm smoking, and he walks by and asks me for a light. Next thing I know it's 6 am and I have around seventeen missed calls from my not-yet husband and I'm not sure where my knickers are but I'm quite certain I wore them to work.'

Jane clapped her hands in excitement.

'This is excellent. I have questions, naturally. First, how did you know it was him? Second, if you were as catastrophically drunk as you describe, how can you be sure you shagged him at all? It could all be a fantasy that you've told yourself over and over until it's solidified in your mind as truth.'

'Thank you, Chief Detective Jane of the Hackney Central Police,' I guffawed. 'Let me explain – wait, are you finishing that?'

'No, you are.'

'Fab,' I said, emptying the share plate onto mine.

A gregarious, tattooed woman popped out from behind the bar and headed towards our table, embracing Jane and kissing her on both cheeks. She announced herself as Lucia.

'This woman, legend of Soho!'

'Well, that title may be transferred after this conversation, Lucia. My new friend here is telling me of a frankly unbelievable sexual conquest.'

Lucia slammed her fist down on the table in approval. 'Fantastico! I bring us all Spritz Termini, and you tell.'

Lucia danced her way back to the service area and turned up the music.

I groaned.

'What's wrong?' Jane said.

'She definitely knows him. They all do.'

'Chrissy?'

'No, my –'

'You never told him?'

'I didn't see the point. It never happened again. Why upset him?'

'I'll reserve my judgement on that front until I hear the story, but I wouldn't worry about Lucia. She's hardly what we would call shy or retiring. If she knew who you were, you'd have heard about it hours ago.'

'Are you sure?'

'Trust me,' Jane said, as Lucia re-emerged with a flourish, carrying a tray crowded with tall blood-orange glasses. 'You're just another customer.'

'. . . so I could tell he was famous because he just had that *aura*, you know? Didn't have to, like, *announce* it or anything, but it was pretty obvious. And we started talking and he was just *so* American and usually I can't *stand* Americans, but there's just something magnetic about him. I don't really remember what we talked about but I did realise at one point that it was getting quite late and I still hadn't told my partner where I was. And that was *after* this supermodel Indian guy with a bull ring through his nose swam up to us, realised who he was and just screamed. It didn't really change anything though; I was still attracted to him, and the idea of putting my hands all over him in some dark corner somewhere in the building had taken root in my mind and then it was all I could think about. Enzo and I had been together for maybe four or five years and all the signs were pointing in one direction, but I wasn't sure I was ready to go there yet. We had this thing we said to each other as a joke: "next year". Like, after this one is done, we'll become adults, buy a property, move out of Central London and really start trying for kids. I think we'd been saying it for a couple of years. But I'd only just hit my thirties and I didn't want it to be the end of my life, you know? I'm not a very out-there person, but I have my dreams and my fantasies and I also have this tendency to throw a pipe bomb into the middle of things when they're going well, like I don't trust it, or I don't trust myself . . .'

I was talking too much. My heart was a printer with a paper jam. I took a breath. Jane and Lucia sat before me, enraptured. Nobody had so much as touched their drinks.

'Anyway, next thing I know it's half-three in the morning or something ridiculous and everyone had emptied out of the pool area and I really, desperately needed to piss out all this gin, so I told Chris – sorry, Michael – that I'd be back in a minute and I made the fastest ever beeline for these cabana bathrooms, and I decided on the way that when I came back, I was going to screw him stupid on the lounge chair and that was the end of that.'

My two new friends stared at me, saying nothing. Eventually, Lucia's engine started back up.

'And the actor, *Sopranos* man, he . . .'

'He'd been very gracious the entire evening. I guess because of his character on the show I was half-expecting him to be all gross and sexist or whatever, and he definitely swore a lot, but he was funny and kind and even though he approached me, he never tried to push himself onto me or anything like that. He was just interested, asked me questions about myself and waited for the answers. In my relationship, I was always the one asking questions. I was the blanks my husband filled in for me because he's the extrovert, always out there living. Blazing like a bloody house fire. I'm more quiet, you know, but I'm not dull. It can kill you to love someone so much, but to feel like the reliable part of his life, not the exciting part. He raved about me, you know, he did right up until he left. But I think there's a big difference between loving someone in the third and first person. That night, Michael made me feel like an "I", you know? I hadn't felt that for such a long time that it just did something instinctual to me. So when I was done in the loo, I hung out there for a few more minutes and I –

'Oh, *shit.*'

'What?' said Jane.

'I've just realised something.'

'Si,' said Lucia, who had followed the story with what seemed to be an uncharacteristic quietness.

My neck was Hades. My face was the surface of the sun. Later, Lucia would go home and prepare puttanesca for her boyfriend out of the pulpy red flesh that once was my skin. I would taste salty, sinful, delicious. The sound her pot of water made as it reached boiling point, ready for the pasta's arrival, would be indiscernible from the rapidly unfurling 'fuuu-uuuu-uuuuu-uuuuuuck' now screaming across my subconscious.

Jane spoke first, gingerly.

'I'm afraid I haven't quite caught up. Fair few Spritzers, you know . . .'

'It's probably for the best, I think.'

How was I even forming words at this point? This had to be the most mortifying moment of my life – and I'd only recently been dumped.

'Whatever it is, I'm sure I did worse in the '80s.'

'I don't know about that, Jane. Did you ever convince yourself that you had thrilling, once-in-a-lifetime early morning sex with a celebrity and then beat yourself up over it for four years when *actually,* all you did was go to the loo and have a furious wank while he waited out there for you, like some absolute idiot?'

'Definitely not what I thought you were going to say,' Jane demurred, fishing the final olive out of the collection of glasses crowding out the table, 'but in a way, it makes the story better, don't you think?'

Though I'd drunk a fair bit by then, I'd definitely eaten far too much. My restricted, recently single diet meant I wasn't accustomed to banging down an entire buffet's worth of rich cheese and cured meats. I zeroed in on this rising indigestion, feeling its punchy, blobbing edges start to take shape in my guts. Anything to distract me from the suddenly crisp scented imprint of cigarettes, Fever Tree tonic and the rapid clip with which I was able to make myself come.

I groaned, lying my head on the last free space on the tiny table, covering my face with my forearm like a five-year-old throwing a tantrum.

'Christ, this is embarrassing.'

'Look at it another way,' Jane said.

'What, like poke my eyes out slowly with these cocktail toothpicks?'

'You said earlier, before you took us on this grand, made-up odyssey, that you weren't in raptures over what you'd done. Cheating on your long-term boyfriend, who would go on to become your husband. I believe the words you used were "not proud of it".'

'That's right. It was a really fucked-up thing to do.'

'But sweetheart,' Jane smiled conspiratorially, 'you never did it. Last I checked, there's no law in this country against touching yourself. You think your husband didn't fire up the computer when you were out late?'

'Is human nature, this thing,' Lucia chimed in. 'Me, I do every afternoon. After lunch and before I come here. Good for nerves, help me relax. Sometimes this place is fucking crazy.'

'I'm sorry,' I pulled myself off the table, pointing to the two women in turn, 'is this really happening? You, I met on the internet – through your daughter. And you I met, what, an hour ago? Did I fall asleep and wake up in a new reality?'

'We were just trying to demonstrate that it's okay,' said Jane. 'You really do look like you're about to go and walk in front of the 43 bus and I just couldn't have that on my conscience.'

'Forza! For strong women!' a voice announced out of nowhere.

Lucia had plugged her phone into the aux cable behind the bar. Within seconds, Chaka Khan's 'I'm Every Woman' was belting out through Termini's speakers. The remaining drinkers on other tables, who I'd completely forgotten even existed, barely registered it. Sudden changes in mood must have been a regular feature here.

Lucia held her hand out to Jane and they spun around the near-empty room, singing and caterwauling into vacant chairs. A tide broke somewhere beneath my ribs. I felt the raspberry-Aperol-Heinz puree slowly drain from my face. It was late. I'd probably already missed the last night bus back to Amhurst Road. But I'd never looked forward more to that slightly terrifying night-time walk in my life.

Lucia had put the song on infinite loop by accident. A few Soho stragglers were peering through the window, likely wondering what on Earth had become of that respectable cocktail bar with their white-smocked waitstaff.

Jane collapsed into the booths, spent.

'You wanted to keep him in the third person,' she panted, fanning herself with a coaster.

'Who?' I shouted back. The music was still feverishly loud.

'Christopher. Michael. Whoever. You wanted him for your own private universe.'

I thought on this for a minute. I considered, for the first time, the possibility of a second act, free of guilt. I contemplated calling Enzo as I walked along the canal after midnight, keys jutting between my fingers for safety, knowing he'd pick up, just to tell him that the terrible thing he never knew I did, I hadn't actually done after all. We'd laugh and I'd tell him I'd just discovered that bar he was always on about but never took me to.

But it was possible I'd maxed out on my quota of strange chats for the evening. The year, even.

Staggering to my feet at last, I hauled the forgotten bounty of Tony, Chrissy and Paulie onto the table. The disco chorus revved up again. Lucia was now serenading an empty Campari bottle.

'Jane!' I yelled over the racket.
I pointed to the bag.
'You owe me 85 quid.'

# INTERMEZZI: CLOSE, BUT NOT QUITE

ENZO REMAINS NEARBY. He is not a monster.

It doesn't matter which borough he finds himself in, which basement flat or shared warehouse on the marshes or short-term cupboard in a fancy new build they gave him at a discount because they hadn't checked if the heating was working properly yet but mostly because he looks like he was hit by a bus that reversed back over him just to make sure his soul was properly crushed.

Enzo remains nearby. He could be anywhere, but why would he be. Fantasies of flight – and we know he's had a few in the nauseating depths of dawn, shivering in a single bed, readjusting his earplugs to drown out his new flatmates having a row or a rave, repeating the invocations his mama had him learn for Mass, back when he had love in his life, so much love where now there's only other people's music pulsating through the walls – they hold no purpose. Enzo is not going anywhere.

The only thing you need to know about Enzo is that he lies in the dark, holding his useless phone aloft, waiting. He bucks and sways on the Central Line, enveloped in the disarming physicality of strangers, opening and closing the text dialogue box. He walks along the canal – it does not matter which one – and if you see him from across the water in the greedy swallowing of dusk, he is a disembodied tussle of hair lit up in a spearmint blue halo.

Enzo has been typing and deleting the same message for six months.

He remains nearby, because he knows that one day it will come to him, almost completely at random as inspired thoughts tend to do, the words he wants to say. Until that time comes, he acquiesces to the reality that this non-communicated communication will stalk him through both his waking and sleeping moments. There are 248 drafts of this message sitting in Enzo's phone, which he has written at the office, in the pub, drinking coffee, while on the phone to his father, waiting for interview subjects or taking a shit. Even when he doesn't have his device, Enzo composes in his mind, arranging his thoughts in two languages, the coolness of English sparring with the white-hot indignation of his native tongue.

It doesn't matter what he writes because it is never right. Enzo has not been this wrong, has not grasped at an answer for this long since he was a boy. He sits at the counter of Bar Termini, staring mindlessly at their array of coloured glass bottles, phone attached to his left hand like a graft. Lucia takes pity on him and feeds him panettone and biscotti, having not yet made the connection that it was his wife who was in here only last week.

Enzo is so single-minded in the pursuit of this perfect message that he begins walking into things. Sometimes they are innocuous, like lampposts, other times they are people, or animals. He walks with his headphones burrowed into his ears and listens to their joint playlist, searching for leads. She has continued updating it, likely out of habit rather than calculation, and he catches glimpses of her mood on delay through the recent additions, strange new artists like Let's Eat Grandma, Goat Girl, someone called Nilüfer Yanya.

Enzo taps out sentences that become paragraphs that become essays. He pleads and he swears and he summons stunning insights as well as terrible metaphors. It is all there, a miasma of anguish splintered and speckled through the graveyard of half-written messages he has not sent. But he can't arrange it in the right way. Enzo has always been an excellent writer; he is the first foreign employee at his agency in twelve years. But editor he is not.

Enzo workshops his message with his sister Sofia, with whom he lives for a spell before appreciating the hard truth that her flat in Clapton is dangerously close to Hackney and he is still too raw, an exposed wire that could trip off an explosion if he even saw a glimpse of Elly. Sofia's English is second-rate at best, but in all matters pertaining to the slashed organ quickly bleeding out inside her brother's chest, she is an expert. She counsels him on his choice of adjectives, the ways in which he repeats himself. More drafts join the heap. If they were bodies, Enzo would have murdered a small Roman legion.

It doesn't matter what he writes, what matters only is that he writes it. The very act of composition, of trying to summon an explanation, an admonishment, a proclamation and a plea, seems to Enzo to be irrefutable proof that the love story which has consumed over half his adult life is not yet over. As long as he is thinking about it, there is a good chance Elly is, too. So Enzo, in new clothes and address, but carrying his old demons, remains nearby.

Having lost access to Andiamo, Enzo takes to riding a stationary bike in the rubberised grimness of his local gym. It in no way replicates the joyousness of gliding through the park; stale recycled air, bad techno music and creatine-emulsified BO. He thrashes himself on the pedals and grits his teeth. Alex from his office, who has recently gone through a similar ordeal, recommends punishing exercise as a means of distraction. Soon Enzo has jelly legs; he loosens the straps on his feet and can barely stand up. But all he sees, all he can think about, is Elly. He wonders if anyone will ever call him 'Darling' again. His limbs give way and he tips onto the floor; he makes no effort to get up. When the ambulance arrives, he doesn't say that this was just an experiment to try and find the thread of what he wants to say, to avoid thinking about who he wants to address it to. He lies on the gurney, pumped full of fluids, torches flashing across his pupils, enjoying the fleeting feeling of being a person that someone else cares about.

Against his better judgement, Enzo does not return home. He does not tell his parents, who always loved Elly even if they found her strange and aloof, that they have split. He does not see the invitations to weddings, the birthday and Christmas cards addressed to them both that start to fade and curl at the edges on the counter at Academy Apartments. He has set up emails from Elly to go straight to spam. Enzo does not realise that Elly has taken a similar approach to his, that most of her friends and family are unaware that they have torn up their future. If he knew, Enzo would probably take cold comfort in the idea that to outsiders their relationship currently loops like a scratched CD, playing only snatches of a happier time.

Enzo ponders the big question, the inflection point. He goes back to the scene, changes his face and stretches the rubber band in other ways to see if it will still snap. He smells the curry, the searing garam masala and bay leaf shrivelling up angrily into ash. He goes out for burgers with workmates, drinks pints of Peroni with interview subjects and tunes out entirely. There is only one channel in Enzo's non-televised mind and it's permanently fixed on 12 July 2018. He watches the argument flare again and again, walking in and around the blow-up like he's at the McKittrick Hotel, experiencing the same play from a million unique vantage points.

Eventually Elly says the words. There is no way around it. The rubber band snaps each and every time. It slaps Enzo in the face and neck and it stings like a motherfucker. It is when he is at his lowest, trying to buy weed on a Tuesday afternoon or watching porn in an office cubicle or eating his third helping of rigatoni at Bancone, the only place Elly's mum ever agreed to go with them because it was in Covent Garden, that it tingles the worst. This rubber band is why Enzo is finding it so hard to conjure the right words even though he arranges them for a living. But Enzo knows the correct phrase exists, even though he doesn't want to think about it. Gwyneth Paltrow used it when she broke up with the guy from Coldplay. The first time he and Elly read it in the *Daily Mail* they laughed at how precocious it was, but now, with only a broken rubber band for company, it starts to make a lot of sense.

'Conscious uncoupling.'

The streets for Enzo are filled with the ghosts of Elly. They slosh their long legs through the muck on rainy days, unafraid of getting their new black boots wet. Translucent Ellys follow him onto the Piccadilly Line, whisper down his neck and stand back to fix the collar of his shirt. They goad him over the litany of messages he will never send. He knows that if he can just put the words together, one of them will be right. All of these phantoms will vanish and, in their place, will be his wife, warm blood pumping through her veins and playing with her fringe and laughing over her second coffee of the morning as they gaze hungrily at one another and discuss the ludicrous vanity of declaring oneself consciously uncoupled.

# V. WAGON

Every young couple in London eventually finds themselves having the Big Three Conversations. These don't necessarily unfold in sequential order; sometimes they flow together after midnight, when one party isn't quite ready to fall asleep, or puncture the silence on lazy Saturday mornings at an always-reliable greasy spoon in Bethnal Green, London Bridge or Clerkenwell. But without fail or fanfare, usually around the three- to five-year mark, they arrive. The moment the view-finder flicks left or right on the lasting imprints of one's life can usually be tracked back to said discussions and Elly, who by virtue of being more deliberate with her choice of words is regularly mistaken for an available agony aunt at work, has heard enough about this phenomenon to know it is true.

So sure is Elly of this eventuality that she jots down the Big Three deep inside the skeuomorphic Notes section of her phone, with noble intentions of returning to tick them off using ironic emojis, only to lose it amid a tidal wave of shopping lists and fleeting observations and addresses of cheap nail salons and lists of films she should watch (but doesn't) and books she should read (but won't) as advised by *The Guardian*, *The Times* and Jess, the only other girl in the office she properly likes.

1. Where will we move to when the city gets too expensive?
2. Do we want to have kids/how many?
3. When are we going to Glastonbury together?

Elly, it has been noted, is not traditionally what a sardonic '90s Los Angeles film narrator would describe as a 'people person'. But this does not preclude her from chasing the universal thrill of being utterly subsumed by a crowd, somewhat purposefully losing her friends, going on meandering adventures through vast fields and rendering herself utterly anonymous amid hundreds and thousands of revellers. Elly first went to Glastonbury with friends from back home when she was seventeen, and despite becoming more reserved and particular about her own tastes, the appeal of the mega-festival has never waned for her. She feels the pull of the tent city as soon as it becomes warm enough to shed winter coats, and remains an active member of a longstanding group chat concerned exclusively with ticket-buying strategy, tent locations, line-up clashes and the pre-purchasing and concealing of MDMA that has survived break-ups, marriages, elopement and the arrival of babies.

2017 will mark Elly's sixth Glastonbury and the first time she's planning on bringing a partner. Enzo typically spends the summer back home in Naples, so she's already gone twice without him. She's managed, not without difficulty, to convey the importance of this ritual to her fiancé, who after much cajoling, agrees to delay his trip home and sign up for the ballot.

The principle of pre-planning for an event that has no confirmed artists and sells out over half a year in advance should be the antithesis of Enzo's usual way of doing things, which after nearly a decade together, Elly has roughly summarised as Let's Just Dive In and See What Happens. But she also knows that Enzo's ability to make these easy judgement calls is offset by his very real desire, baked into the same part of his brain that makes him financially hyper-literate, to fully understand the variables of any situation before it might arise. His outward spontaneity is always the result of ruthless advance calculation, which, if taken out of his hands, manifests as anxiety.

Glastonbury, with its myriad Choose Your Own Adventure outcomes, poses something of an issue for Enzo, who is still very much in love with Elly, perhaps more so than ever, but quietly terrified of that which he cannot effectively prepare for. While this sits in stark contrast to his continual presence at wild underground grime shows, in these instances, Enzo has typically mapped out his transport options, where and when he will eat, pre-ordered himself a taxi back home and tried on three different pairs of shoes before even stepping through the venue's weed-shrouded front entrance. It does not take Elly long to realise that Enzo's love of chaos is firmly underpinned by his need for control, which he rarely imposes on her but inflicts ruthlessly upon himself.

As a child in Naples during the late '80s, there was no word yet for this curiosity, and even now, Enzo's character eludes standard psychological classification. He is, if Elly were to summarise it, a highly functioning, extremely sociable neurotic. As a notorious overachiever, many of these traits have blended naturally into his regular personality and are hard to isolate as problematic. In any event, it causes her absolutely no bother 98 per cent of the time and seems to have had minimal impact on Enzo's life, aside from triggering brief spells of depression which he bats off in conversation to the point of triviality and never explicitly names.

Having successfully acquired himself a pass, with Elly's northern cabal working him into their elaborate spreadsheet effortlessly before taking on the ticketing platform with hitman-like precision, Enzo veils his nervousness under the cheery guise of a hapless foreigner asking standard questions about this bastion of British debauchery.

It is October 2016. Elly and Enzo change into their joggers and stroll through Hackney Downs, a park not nearly as aesthetically pleasing as Victoria, or even London Fields, but closer, and quiet enough on weeknights to feel like it is theirs. They used to walk hand in hand, Elly self-conscious about their height difference, but now they loop arms like an old couple, Enzo always on the left and always the overarm link in the chain, tactfully intertwining them while dialling down any awkwardness. Subtleties like this, which seem to come naturally to Enzo, remind Elly of why she loves him when she is more regularly predisposed to be annoyed with him. They have, by millennial standards at least, been together for a very long time. But there remains something classic about the two of them.

The local Rasta rides by in a slow-moving cloud of skunk, crackly Bluetooth speaker blaring a reggae doppler of Bob Marley's 'Three Little Birds'. Enzo smirks, feigning elitism, though in reality he is catastrophically worried.

'So, this festival,' he begins cautiously.

'I can't believe we got you in! It's going to be amazing, I'm so bloody excited.'

'Si, me too. So, you might need to explain some things to me. To help, you know.'

'I am the expert, you are the novice. It is my duty, nay, my privilege, to induct you into this glorious event.'

'To sleep, we are in tents?'

'Yep. We know where all the good spots are by now, so we'll camp next to the others, as a group.'

'But how do you find it again, there's many people.'

'Look, you'll get lost a few times.'

'Lost?'

'Not *lost* lost, just a bit muddled. It's just an absolutely massive place. It's hard to describe, really. Every time you think you've hit the edge it just keeps going.'

'Okay, so I stick with you and we have each other.'

'Well I hope you weren't planning on leaving me at the entrance!'

By this juncture, Elly has amassed significant experience with the spiky undercurrent to Enzo's performative extroversion. Her method to date has been to play things down, or better yet, take the piss out of herself. Most of the time it works. As they reach the corner by The Star pub and head for their favourite path, beneath bending rows of London plane trees, she does the mental arithmetic of just how bad this could get if she doesn't take the right approach. All the while, Enzo spits out questions like he's on autopilot.

'How do we get there?'

'Do we drive or catch the bus or what?'

'They search us for drugs?'

'How do you know which stage is where?'

'How far is the walk to the campsite?'

'What happens if it rains?'

'What happens if it's really hot?'

'Can you leave early?'

'Is there reception?'

'How do we charge our phones?'

'How will we carry everything in?'

She feels his arm muscles tense, still coiled around hers. Elly and Enzo don't ever talk about this quirk in his personality – at least not head-on in the way the pamphlets and websites tend to advise. Elly lets her mind wander as they walk, imagining briefly that in the sitting room of one of these houses bordering the park, the local chapter of Outgoing Types With Crippling

Anxiety Anonymous is having their weekly meeting, members so desperately over-gregarious that progress seems impossible, like travelling to a far-off planet.

'What time does the music start?'

'What do we eat every day?'

'What if I lose you?'

Elly is many things, but worrisome has never been one of them. Since her parents split up when she was still very young, she's adopted the default position of assuming the worst – or at the very least, a negative outcome – from almost every situation. She has always seen this as an intelligent form of expectation setting. During a recent team-building exercise, when her bosses had wheeled in some flashy advisor to the likes of Burberry and Fred Perry to help them bond better as a team, she'd filled in a standardised personality quiz only to discover that she possessed a 'fixed mindset'. The way that walking eating disorder with teeth had tut-tutted at her made it seem like Elly was on the losing side of life, backing the team at the bottom of the league table. Rather, she'd seen it as a form of undeniable validation; that she liked what she liked, was robust in both her opinions and ideas and that frequently, other people could be susceptible, flip-floppy morons. It is this same mindset that makes it difficult for Elly to catastrophise, or empathise with those who do. Before meeting her, Enzo had probably dealt with these panicked thoughts internally. *The joy of long-term, monogamous partnerships*, she sighs to herself.

During less fraught moments, Enzo and Elly have discussed the glaring discrepancy at the heart of their romantic entanglement; that while he dove into this relationship without even checking the depth of the ocean floor, she has always carved out parts of herself to which he'll never be allowed access. What frustrates Elly the most about Enzo's nervous fluttering, aside from how decidedly unbecoming it is on a man who generally spreads sex appeal around like Lurpak on toast, is that Glastonbury is without doubt one of these secret chambers of hers. She is inviting him in, something she has deliberately avoided with past partners, and his response is to go into a tailspin. Elly does not need to consult with her old lot from Stockport to know that relationships that last are built on shared experiences. It is no longer enough for her to get absolutely sideways, stumble into a field and dance to some DJ she's never even heard of until sunrise; she now wants to do all of these things with him.

'And if you want to see one artist, but I want to see other artist, how do we –'

'Darling . . .' she cuts him off. They are approaching an empty bench, and she drags him onto it. 'Nothing bad is going to happen. This thing has been running for nearly fifty years. It's not some illegal rave in a forest. It's really well organised.'

'Si, but –'

'Listen,' she says, putting her hand on his thigh, which she already knows will be shaking uncontrollably. 'I didn't mention this before, but you can drive there. So how about we do that? We can borrow your sister's car, arrive when we want and even leave early, if that's what you want to do.'

Enzo knows an olive branch when he sees one. He is from Italy, after all.

'For me, you do this?'

'Of course, Darling. I want you to have the greatest time. That's all I care about.'

'E le amiche? They take the coach . . .'

Elly laughs, if a little overenthusiastically.

'I'm in my mid-thirties. I think I've probably done my time on that bleeding bus.'

He thinks on it. The way Darling's mind works is like giving a hamster some Class A's and shoving their wheel inside the monitors at Fabric.

'We still stay with friends, but we drive.'

'Yes.'

'And the stuff; the tent and chairs and beer and clothes and sleeping bags?'

'We carry it in. It's all part of the experience!'

'Si, but . . .'

Elly has been counting these up quietly as she watches the park fade to dark. Five more 'Si, buts' and she figures she's just about earned that black silk bomber from Goodhood that she's been talking herself out of buying all season.

'This is your last question before I get cross, so make it a good one.'

Enzo has been tapping furtively on his phone, which he now passes over to her, blue light radiant against the receding dusk.

'You take coach, stop here.' He points at a star on last year's map, which the legend, once zoomed in enough to be legible, denotes as FESTIVAL ENTRY.

'Car park different, no?'

Elly pinches back out of the graphic to bring it back to its original size and scrolls up. Very far up. She has to concede this is a valid point. It's fucking miles away and there's a lot of stuff to haul in, especially without twelve of her nearest and dearest sharing the load between them.

'Darling,' she says. 'Are you ready to go to my second favourite store on Earth?'

It's not that she's a particularly outdoorsy type of woman – quite the opposite really. But having been dragged to the sprawling superstore as a teenager with her pa after he decided that becoming a Middle-Aged Man in Lycra would help win back his ex-wife, and spent every weekend in here sourcing more biking kit, she fell in love with the audacity of the place, the unwieldy everythingness of it. 'Like a useful IKEA,' she tells Enzo as they schlep out to Chingford on their mission to find a collapsible wagon and about six other completely unnecessary camping items that they will use a grand total of once. With most large-scale retailers rapidly moving online, Elly's weird fetish for gigantic, multi-aisle barns stuffed with esoteric adventure, fishing, gym and sports kit seems remarkably anachronistic. It is 2016, or Year Nine of Our Lord, Amazon Prime Same-Day Delivery; she could have just as easily ordered the thing, all neatly packed in foam and cardboard, straight to the Academy's double doors. Instead, they're spending Saturday morning battling an unreliable overground line and bus connection so they can argue loudly about the purchase in person.

Elly has always viewed a Decathlon marathon as the starting gun for the onset of Glastonbury season and so relishes an outing she'd otherwise work overtime to avoid. The train approaches Walthamstow Central. A throng of sequinned, over-glittered young women, clearly still going from the night before, spill into the carriage, collapsing onto the spare seats and each other. In the midst of their very public comedown, a few of them smile at Enzo, who has given up his seat for an older man and is curiously gazing in their direction like they're some sort of anthropological experiment.

*Bloody hell,* Elly thinks. *This man could probably pull in a morgue.*

As predicted, the wagon is an absolute ball ache to bring home. The box is just heavy and odd-sized enough that lugging it onto a bus or out of the station requires both of them each time. Elly's enthusiasm peters out halfway home when her grip gives out and the box cannonballs down a flight of stairs on the 149, nearly killing an elderly Ghanaian woman. Enzo, meanwhile, immediately adds the chunkiness of the apparatus to his growing list of potential disasters that could unfold come June bank holiday weekend. When they finally get back to the flat, they shove the box in the corner and go straight across the road to the pub, and for the rest of the afternoon Enzo works overtime to hold his tongue, aware that this is not the time for machine-gun questioning regarding festival logistics.

*

There are many things going on in his life that Enzo doesn't talk much about during that incoming spring, but mostly it's the growing fear that he's just entered a new demographic, the '18–30' bracket having disappeared fully in the rear-view, with not a whole lot to show for it. Nobody has more unrealistic expectations than Enzo has for himself; raised to be a winner, having triumphantly escaped his city and country of origin, having conquered Heathrow, Lloyd's Bank, Pret A Manger, now, at the time in his life when he should be the most content with his lot, he finds himself flatlining ingloriously. Elly had always thought it was wrapped up in what her fiancé did for a living. Spending your time interviewing that many people with that much money, she tells her hairdresser, it can't be healthy. These men – and they are almost always men – spend more on lunch than Elly and Enzo do on rent for the month. They pay people to plant secret money seeds in rich soil utterly devoid of tax, and fertilise it with more money, growing their wealth exponentially as they sleep.

The days start to draw out again, afternoons emerging from winter duvets of all-consuming darkness, but Elly registers that Enzo has become less enthusiastic to meet them. Suggestions of aperitivo hour with store-bought cocktails and 2-for-1 antipasto pots that typically accompany the very first hint of clear skies are exchanged for another night in front of the TV, bingeing some series that Elly's mum has insisted they watch but that they only have a passing interest in. Dreading the monotony, and completely at a loss for how best to handle this growing concern that is her partner, who is close to mute for the first time in the eight years she has shared her life with him, Elly does the unthinkable and actively stays late at work. She whiles away those yawning hours between 5.30 pm and sleep adjusting presentations; moving hypothetical furnishings around rendered rooms and methodically running through every combination of wood grain and countertop stone and carpet colour and doorhandle shape and sofa fabric and light-bulb wattage until each proposal is perfect. Her escapism is mistaken for diligence and for the first time in her life, Elly is awarded not only a bonus, but a promotion. She doesn't tell Enzo about it, and he never asks. The bomber jacket she has coveted for so long sits limply in its bag by the door. She considers taking it back.

The penny finally drops when the full line-up does. In any other circumstance, Elly could safely expect Enzo to absolutely lose his mind at the gigantic list of performers they'll be seeing come June, which she can't help but notice includes some of his favourite MCs of all time. Stormzy, Dizzee, JME, Skepta, Wiley . . . these are rappers he's been devoutly following and privately chronicling since he moved to London. He has a drawer overflowing with ticket stubs, bootleg 7-inches, rum-splattered set lists and loud, oversized merch he only wears when exercising. His YouTube favourites collection, documenting every corner of the scene, from pre-career freestyles to home-made docos and fan footage, could easily populate a museum. He never shuts up about these guys and from what Elly can gather, it even looks like some of them are headlining stages, which is a huge coup. Elly waits all day for the text in all caps, punctuated by too many exclamation marks that is the hallmark of Italian thought patterns parsed back into English. Her group chat explodes with excitement, but not Enzo.

His depression – if that is truly what this is, and in Elly's entirely unprofessional opinion, the jury is still out – isn't a one day to the next thing. It disembowels Enzo quietly, scratching at internal scabs without leaving any visible marks, so expert at camouflage that some days he seems his regular self. It has been six months since the park bench showdown, and on balance, he seems to be getting worse. It's no longer just the festival itself. It's the prospect of attacking life with any semblance of zeal that seems entirely beyond him, with Glastonbury standing in for a general sense of failure. Elly finds this increasingly distressing, having operated from the baseline assumption, frequently validated by Enzo, that this was something under his control. But she now understands his mood has traversed new depths where she cannot safely swim. Enzo, it has been said, has always been short. But to Elly, this is the first time he feels small.

Over risotto that evening, Elly marvels aloud at how many of Enzo's favourites will be playing the Other and West Holts stages in a mere matter of months.

'It's like they cut open your head and just scooped it out of your brain,' she says, scraping the bowl with her spoon to get the last few grains of rice. 'You must be well up for it.'

Enzo's upper body is crunched over his plate. His neck and head have receded into his strong shoulders. It is like he is trying to transform into a tortoise in real time.

'Si,' he says softly. 'Very cool.'

He returns to playing with his food, which he's barely touched, and refilling his glass, which he's done several times.

Elly appreciates silence more than the average person, but in that moment, she has officially found her litmus.

'Darling, I think we need to talk about what's going to happen this summer.'

'I . . .'

He isn't looking at her, but Elly can tell Enzo is cracking up. He does this thing where his voice barely modulates, tears sneaking their way out of his ducts, but eventually that nose betrays him.

On Elly's crumbling digital radio, volume turned down to background level, the inescapably hooky chorus of Justin Bieber's 'Sorry' splutters through the static.

'I . . .'

'Just tell me. Please.'

'I give up my ticket already. For resale. I'm so sorry, I can't. I think I need some help, maybe?'

Elly never knows what to do in these situations, but for once, her aching soul jumps in front of her brain. The metal chair scrapes against the wood and falls to the floor as she makes a beeline around the unnecessarily large table for Enzo, her man. She wraps him in her arms, in her body and holds him as he shudders and convulses. To an outsider, it would seem like she is trying to exorcise something from inside of him, something poisonous. Elly holds her Darling until he calms down. She whispers to him, over and over again. Finally, he lifts his head, eyes meeting hers for the first time that evening. And for a millisecond, a tiny glimmer, Elly can put a face to the parasite that has taken over her fiancé's nervous system. It terrifies her.

Somewhere in that flash of a moment, Elly glimpses an alternate, discordant future for herself. She appreciates, perhaps properly for the first time, that while this has so far been a relatively isolated incident in their relationship, it's unlikely to be the last. Briefly and selfishly, she wonders if she really has the mettle to carry Enzo through these passages of listlessness as he has so often done for her. He is her everything, that man, but now it seems he can be two men. Nobody signs up for this, she thinks as she rubs her hands across Enzo's back to soothe him. But also, there is nobody like him. Even at his worst, he is still worth it.

Elly recalls a conversation she had with her pa when she was in her final year of school, about her mother who left and how neither of them saw it coming.

'There's just no training to be had for it,' he'd said, passing her the tub of Häagen-Dazs with the spoon stuck in as they sat together in the empty kitchen.

'Life, that's all you get. You live it and then you know.'

Soon, Enzo is no longer the only person crying in Flat 36 of Academy Apartments. From her safe vantage point on the purple Chesterfield, upon which she has been curled up the entire evening, Lola watches her adopted guardians embrace, but in a way she hasn't seen before. They hold each other for longer than is necessary, longer than could be considered comfortable. Lola wonders if the humans are sick, or if they are using one another for support. She meows delicately, then more insistently, but they seem not to hear her. Later, when they have finished the wine and gone to bed with all their clothes still on, she will devour Enzo's cold risotto with relish, searching for clues.

**Penny Williams 05.09**
**Hi, is this still available?**

Who knew offloading a brand-new wagon would be such an ordeal? Fuck Penny and the Škoda she rode in on.

'Whadja mean, you haven't opened it?'

'We never used it.'

'You didn't even take it out of the box to try it?'

'No, I bought it at the store. Saw one in action on the floor. I know how it works.'

'I don't understand. Is something wrong with it? You're selling it for so cheap I just assumed it were second-hand.'

'Just a really good bargain,' I said through gritted teeth.

'Marketplace, you just expect used shite, d'you know what I mean?'

'Yes, there's a fair bit of junk on there.'

'And the people . . .' she said, without a hint of irony. 'Absolute freakshow.'

Penny never stood a chance because she'd arrived a full twenty minutes early. God, I detest people like that, always trying to prove something with their virtuous punctuality. A note to all you holier-than-thou prompt people: the other party will still be late. This is London, not Zurich. We build delays in like they do for live radio hosts that swear too much. There is always a contingency for running a bit behind. You get no extra points for beating the clock.

I'd arrived back at Academy after work with a bulging Sainsbury's bag that clinked a bit too much for a Tuesday evening, not expecting visitors because again, nobody was meant to be here yet. When I first saw Penny pacing back and forth in the cobbled laneway, I'd assumed she was just another lost girl jonesing for a fix. Dealers and pimps loved using our long drive to dispense gear or check in on their local runners. While the day-to-day tenants of Academy Apartments had become somewhat fancier in the years since it was a functioning school, the surrounding estates had not benefited from any of the halo effects. Enzo and I would often get home after work and see blacked-out BMWs or Audis idling at the threshold where Institute Place met Amhurst Road, a no-man's-land I liked to call Chicken Shop Run. Getting from Dixy Chicken past our favourite kebab spot and the nail salon that also seemed to be a front for something nefarious – we'd genuinely never once seen those shutters open – down the lane and through the first gate was a gauntlet run at the best of times. The chances of the area being calm, or relatively safe for that matter, were highly variable.

As it transpired, Penny was just fuelled by relentless Young Mum Energy, an endlessly renewable source that accounted for her impatience and forthrightness, but not for being generally awful. Penny had meals to plan, pick-up times to organise. Penny was only a year older than me – I know this because she asked my age within two minutes of accosting me outside my own building – but already had three children. Penny alternately referred to her kids – all under the age of five, including an unplanned-for chaser of Irish twins – as bloodsuckers, ratbags and terrorists. In the midst of this, she took the time to ask, with the sort of tact that I imagine so endeared her to absolutely nobody, why I didn't have any. Penny was someone I could never imagine as a Penelope. She was not someone who had faded from grace, was once elegant or kind or carefree. Penny was someone in the midst of writing the world's longest sob story, which she'd unofficially started composing in the A&E the night she'd pushed out her first bloodsucker and would continue in a long, epistolatory fashion until she died.

'This is the 10L one, then.'

She stood in front of the sealed box, which I'd moved to the entry alcove. I'd had enough experience with Marketplace by now to actively safeguard against inviting just anybody in.

'That's what it says, yep.'

'And the wheels, you'll vouch for them? I'm not lugging this bastard all the way to Crete and paying the extra baggage tax just for it to go to shit on the first walk down to the beach.'

You know that aunt everyone has that matches her lipstick to her nail polish to her hair and shoes? It's like they pick one shade and that becomes their theme for the month, like a bad Pantone Colour of the Year voted for exclusively by other aunts?

Anyway, Penny's was fuchsia.

'I mean, I tried it out at Decathlon and it seemed pretty sturdy.'

'Aye, when was that though,' she asked, snapping her gum loudly because if you're going to be fucking abominable, why not do it all at once.

'We bought it for Glastonbury 2017, so around two years ago.'

I realised my mistake before it was out of my mouth. The purple disco machine at the doorway didn't miss it either.

'*We* . . .'

I desperately grasped at ways to pivot away from the subject.

'Sooooo . . . why Crete? Fair way to go with three little monsters, isn't it?'

Penny groaned, barely disguising her ecstatic pleasure at the opportunity to once more bitch about her personal life with a complete stranger.

'Hubby is from down Dorset way and he gets a bit aggy if he isn't by the water come summertime. Personally, I don't get it, bloody sand up yer crack, eyes stinging from the salt and all that. But he makes the money and I just keep a trio of parasites alive every day, so I guess he gets what he wants.'

I'd never met anyone with such contempt for a life so many others seemed to desperately want. It wasn't just a complaint. It was an entire state of mind, shrouded in offensively loud colours.

'Sounds terrible,' I said.

'We only live next to the bloody Lido in Brockwell. The fascination with Europe I'll never understand. No air conditioning, mind. Or lifts. I told him, it's like a third-world country over there.'

'Bit like Glastonbury, really.'

'2017, that's the year they had Sheeran headlining? Some of my mothers' group friends all went together, left the bastards with the husbands for a change. Said he was incredible.'

'So I heard.'

'Shame you two missed it,' she said, indelicately craning her neck around the corner alcove, trying to find traces of another person. Nosy bitch.

'Oh, I didn't. I just wasn't at Ed's set. Bit obvious, I thought. Not like I needed to hear "Shape of You" for the 10,000th time.'

Penny stared at me like my head was exploding with volcanic pus.

'I can't be sure, you know, because I was absolutely off my tits on ketamine, but I think we saw Justice instead.'

I was being mean-spirited, but Penny had cleaned out my bank of Fucks Left To Give and now the available balance was hovering somewhere close to zero. I countered her gaze, putting my hands firmly on the box. I'd keep the damn thing just to spite her at this point.

'Why didn't you take the wagon?' she said.

'What does that –'

'You bought it for the festival, ya went to the festival. So why didn't ya take it? What's wrong with it? Is it, like, defective or summat?'

'Christ! It's a bloody wagon! Four wheels, two crossbars, fabric. It does exactly what it's supposed to do.'

Why I bothered rising to Penny's bait still haunts me. The woman had three children with whom she clearly relished bickering every minute of the day, not to mention any of her own blood relatives still unlucky enough to be in contact with her. This was a sport to her – and I was well out of practice.

'How would you know? It's still in the box.'

'Penny, seriously.'

'He left you, is that it?'

'No,' I said.

'Still on the scene, then.'

'Yes. He's just out. Works late.'

'The wagon his? He know you're selling it?'

'It's ours. And of course he does. What are you insinuating? Did you come all the way out here just to torment someone you don't even know?'

Thank God for the height advantage. In that moment, face reddening and voice rising, I must have come across as quite threatening to Penny. I was easily twice her size. I watched as she reflexively took it down a notch, backing further into the entry nook.

'I'm sorry. You're right. Yer break-up is none of my business.'

'What are you talking about?' I was practically shouting. 'I told you, he's at work!'

'Look love, I wasn't born yesterday. You're sporting a pretty fresh tan line on yer finger where I take it there was recently a shiny little diamond . . .'

'Right, that's it. Out of my house.'

'Nothing to be ashamed of, that. Before I had the little

psychopaths, I'd broken off an engagement and been through a divorce. Just a fact of life these days. Not like our parents. Stayed together through all that wank.'

I started to close the door, forgetting the wagon was wedged in the way. The only method was to force it out, and Penny with it. But that would give her unfettered access to the item I was now hellbent on keeping. It looked like both of us were trapped.

Penny kept blathering on, as was her birthright. But I'd tuned out a while ago, trying to arrange the thoughts in my head that would lead to the killer blow, necessitating her exit. It was like trying to do frontline strategy while under heavy fire. I didn't even see her stop for breath.

'All marriages are just things we do for other people, when ya think on it properly. Who wants to shag the same git for the rest of time? No thanks. My first, complete dud. Used to call him Gone In Sixty Seconds. Not to his face, mind, he had a terrible temper and could really let loose with the fists after a few . . .'

'SSRIs,' I cut in, barely squeezing in between her word avalanches. 'Do you know what they are?'

'SS . . . that some Nazi thing?'

'No, Penny. It's a drug. It boosts your serotonin when you can't produce it yourself. They give it to people that are depressed. Like my husband.'

Penny's eyes widened, like she'd cracked the Rosetta Stone.

'So he is real, then.'

'Very real, and very much not coming home late from work because, as you picked it, we've separated.'

'Oh love,' Penny said. 'Because he's depressed? Men like that, they just drag you down, don't they? You're still so young . . .'

'We're the same age.'

'Look at me. I've run me race. Got the man I wanted; the parasites, the pebble beach vacation where they squeeze lemon all over the bloody grub. But you. You've got yer looks. And them legs. Surprised you haven't put in a take-a-number system for all them lads out there wanting a go at you.'

Short of being eaten alive by piranhas, there is surely nothing as excruciating as being sincerely complimented by someone you despise. It was practically impossible to slam the door shut on Penny now. I had the gnawing sensation that she was about two breaths away from declaring us 'sisters'.

'Anyway,' I said, 'that's not exactly what happened.'

'Doesn't matter though, does it? Yer still on yer own either way, meal pots for one. Grim.'

'I quite like it on my own.'

'They all say that, don't they? "Oh, I prefer me own company." "Oh, I love having time to myself." My aunt went on like that for years until she found a man. Sounded like she had a screw loose. Never spouts that shite anymore, now that she's got a big hairy fella to share a bed with . . .'

And with that, a way out of this train wreck revealed itself in the darkened back alleys of my mind.

'Listen, Penny. That reminds me, there's something I didn't tell you. The wagon . . . it's missing a few screws.'

'Few what?'

'You put it together with screws and bolts, that's how the

wheels attach to the frame. But when we built it, they were missing two. We called and asked for replacements, but they never sent them, and since my husband never ended up coming to Glastonbury anyway, we didn't bother chasing it up.'

'The depressed one.'

'That's right.'

'How can you be too depressed to see Ed Sheeran? He's the king of uplifting music. I listen to him whenever I want to imagine a time before I had all the lunatics.'

'It wasn't really garden-variety sad stuff. He just couldn't do anything. You know when you see old people sort of standing still in the street, like they're not sure how they got there or what they're supposed to do?'

'Aye. Always wonder if a geezer is about to have a stroke.'

'That's what his depression was like. Paralysing. He wasn't sad, he was stuck.'

'Must've been hard on you.'

'Was, yeah. But at least I didn't drag a wagon all the way out to the other end of England just to find out it didn't work.'

Something flickered behind the indigo rims of Penny's bloodshot eyes. It was the look I was banking on: righteous indignation.

'So you mean to tell me that yer trying to offload faulty goods?'

'That's about the size of it. It's a bitch to have hanging around and I figured someone else could probably fix it.'

'But yer didn't say that!'

'Didn't say what?'

'On the ad! Yer didn't say it were missing a few screws. That's important information, that.'

'I guess it is,' I chuckled feebly. 'Maybe I've got a few screws loose, too.'

Penny's face went red, then blue, eventually settling on a purple that matched everything else she was wearing. Her neck expanded, lizard-like, as if she had been secretly hiding gills. It had finally happened. I had turned her into Grimace.

I closed my eyes and waited for her wave of abuse to crash over me.

Instead, I opened them to find her gone. She'd wedged the wagon back inside the door, which had miraculously swung itself shut.

If you could call this winning, I had won.

It was close to ten that night when I texted Himesh.

*Hey Mr Compassionate, how's my table getting on?*

*Elly! How are you? It's great!*

There was a brief ellipsis and then a set of photos popped up on my screen. They were all selfies, Himesh with his parents, his wife and the kids, all crowded around after dinner. It was sickeningly cute. I was torn between throwing my phone at the wall and asking if I could come over for a meal if it wasn't too much of an imposition.

Instead, as was my nature, I wrote something glib.

*Did you just have these sitting there waiting for me to text you?*

*Figured if you were gonna reach out it'd be because you wanted it back, so thought I'd build my case lol*, he fired back.

*Actually, I've got something else you might want. And free, if you want to pick it up.*

*Hope it isn't the fkn fridge.*

I chuckled to myself. *Nope. Wagon. Decathlon. You can put your girls in it on the weekend and roll around the park.*

*I'm listening.*

*There's no sell. It's still in the box. 10L.*

*Could take it to the markets?*

*Throw it off Tower Bridge for all I care. Just get it out of my house*, I typed furiously.

*Why would I throw my kids off a bridge?*

*Met someone just now who I think would actually do that.*

*You're bloody strange. I'll come by at the weekend. I want my kids to meet you.*

Closing the messages, I toggled over to Spotify.

It was time to crank some Sheeran.

# INTERMEZZI: I DO

THE AFTERNOON OF Elly and Enzo's wedding is overcast. It's spitting a bit, nothing crazy, just your average London afternoon; almost as if the entire contraption cranking up there, trying to push out the faintest sniff of sunshine, has completely given up the ghost. Jack, the homeless man who variously lives underneath the arches between Hackney Central and Hackney Downs overground stations, leans out from under his sleeping bag and eyes the sky wearily.

'Don't fancy myself a mechanic but I know a few things about the weather, the main point being that only those with some means ever even notice it,' he says aloud to an audience of a few devoted pigeons. 'When you live in the thick of it, as I have for many a season now, the rain is like the sun is like the wind, which is to say it won't ruin your shoes any more than walking the canals and park all day trying to cobble a few coins together to find a roof, or at least enough Magners to function as such, if you get me. Winter boots all year round, anyhow. Found it to be a bit of a pain keeping trainers together with the slush and the grime and all that.' A 38 bus roars past, scaring most of the birds away. Deep in thought, Jack barely even registers the fluttering.

There's a JD Sports near the Iceland where a few of Jack's fellow downtrodden sometimes hang out in the afternoon, not because they particularly like one another but rather, in the absence of any other human kindness, sometimes it pays to drink yourself senseless with your own kind. Having felt the sudden urge to stretch his legs and sensing no further avian assemblage, this is where Jack soon finds himself. He stares through the gleaming glass window, which is full of new, shiny white trainers.

'White, in London!' he says to Silvio, who appears suddenly in the reflection behind him. Silvio lives in a nook by the stage door up the road at Hackney Empire, which is frequently turned over by the council. 'Never in my forty-nine years. That's wealth, if you ask me. White in a place like this. I can still remember this borough all being factories and the like. Soot and grit. White trainers. For the love of Pete.'

When they've finished their third can and Lou won't sneak them any more out of the service entrance on account of her nearly being fired last Christmas, Jack and Silvio trundle up the old Mare to where the town hall sits. 'Magnificent building, that,' Silvio says, as he says every day. 'Truly,' Jack agrees, as he does every day.

There's a fair few vagabonds hanging about in the square in front of the steps, mostly in search of some action to tide them over until they realise they're still out on the street another night. The realisation sometimes takes a while, even for seasoned ones like Jack, who often likens it to running at the closing doors on the Tube, knowing he won't make it but thinking that maybe if he pushes a bit harder, he'll open his eyes and he'll be inside in the light and the warmth.

Magic.

Sometimes they catch a wedding up here. Jack loves a wedding.

'Don't see happy folk that much around these days, always harrumphing about, too busy to smile at anyone,' he says. Silvio nods, checking the pavement for half-smoked cigarettes that are still good.

'Scared of getting a bit of grime on them white trainers, I suppose. But weddings, my. It's like sunlight. They stand there on the steps, the young ones with their flowers and suits and dresses . . .'

There's nothing nicer than cheerful people, Jack thinks, out there with their family and friends and all spiffy, doing their frozen laughs for the photographer crouching down in front. Even with Howard and Lizzie and some of the other regulars yelling all kinds of stoned nonsense in their direction, they just float above it all.

'I'm not above all that, you know,' he continues monologuing. 'I was married once.'

Silvio has heard this story about as often as he has remarked on how magnificent the town hall facade is. He now realises that he has misplaced his lighter. Perhaps he never had one.

'When I think about her, some of the air comes out of my lungs like a siphon. Don't do it often. I'm not in the best of health, you see. It could kill me.'

Despite his sudden pangs of loneliness and the general bleakness of the weather, Jack is in buoyant spirits. Stephen the community service worker has just come round and said there is an opening. He and Silvio are guaranteed a bed for a few nights. Behind him, he hears a whooping and then some smattered clapping that becomes louder and more jubilant, and his first thought is that maybe they've turned over the residents and they're all getting rooms, but it occurs to him in the moment that it's actually a wedding procession. The happy couple is sailing up the old Mare, the pair of them, dressed all fancy but walking underneath the one umbrella like it could be any other day.

Jack can guess why the lads are cheering. He and Silvio clock the pair immediately. The little Italian fellow who always stops and shouts them a coffee or a lager, depending on the time of day. Knows him and the regulars by name, a fact he's always had an appreciation for. The lass, too. Elly. Stand-offish, as the tall ones sometimes are, but you wouldn't know it to talk to her. They've always commented on the height difference, sometimes in lascivious terms, but that's just how old boys are sometimes; nothing unseemly meant by it.

There's something quite dignified about them walking

themselves up to the chapel, as it were. Regal even. No luxury car waiting to pick them up or big throng of hangers-on. Just a Hackney couple on their way to a Hackney local to tie the knot. That's how Jack and Agnes did it, back then. But like he says, he doesn't like to talk about it.

'Unartificial,' Silvio will later declare as they're sharing the remains of a rollie. 'That's what that was.'

Now, Jack is not a fashion man, per se, but despite his current circumstances, he's been known to have a keen eye for the finer things, his mother having been a seamstress in the glamour days.

'I'll tell you something for free,' he whispers to Lizzie, who has appeared beside him with a fresh can of Stella to share, 'that there is a *dress*.'

For one thing, there's detailing on it the likes of which you'd only ever see in a museum.

'Feathers,' Silvio offers apropos of nothing after she sails past. 'Feathers and lace.'

For another, it's cut off just above the knees, showing off those lovely calves of hers, with a trail coming off from her back. But all that's beside the point, really, the point being that the dress is black. Dead of midnight, jet black. Big boots on too, chunky stompers you wouldn't want your face anywhere near. Also black.

Intrigued, the ramshackle gaggle follows them up to the building where they're to be wed, because it isn't every day you see something of that nature. And what Jack in particular finds quite charming is that the clapping and general carrying on, which they are now very much in the business of doing as a sort of unofficial street entourage, seems to be getting louder as they go. The volume isn't coming from the townsfolk, as one would expect, but from the filth. It appears Jack and his friends are not unique among the lowlife community in being acquainted with Enzo and Elly, and they're all coming out from the off-licences and the pawn shops to cheer them on, the skunkheads and street dealers clapping Enzo on the back and he doesn't mind, even though he's wearing a beautiful forest-green three-piece that to Jack looks very expensive judging by the way it sits on the body, and by the time they get to the steps it's pandemonium and Silvio is of the opinion that in all this excitement, someone might call the cops.

You can imagine the amusement of the wedding party, which seems to number only a handful, most of them looking like the groom's sort with these strong Mediterranean features, to see this procession of degenerates delivering their loved ones to their big moment. Jack, Silvio, Lizzie and the rest must look a real sight, dancing at the foot of the stairs in the sprinkling grey weather, breaking into a chorus of 'All You Need Is Love' with their broken souls and missing teeth. Silvio attempts a cartwheel and lands flat on his back, laughing at the elation of it all.

'And all I am wishing is that the sun will pop out for them, just for a wee minute,' Jack will recount to Agnes later in their scheduled afternoon chat by the big old tree in London Fields. 'Give 'em something pretty. Nice people deserve nice things, you always said – bless your heart.'

But it does not seem forthcoming, in fact potentially the opposite, and soon Elly and Enzo are making designs to head inside and get the show on the road. Elly is standing a bit to the side with her one or two guests and apparently no parents. In fact, Jack doesn't see anyone of his generation in attendance at all. It looks as if she's crying. Even in all this black, that makes her seem very Mary Queen of Scots-ish. Caught up in the romance, he supposes, or maybe something else.

Then the thunder starts to rumble and right on cue, the enforcement officers show up in force, as if the rain won't be washing them all out anyway. Elly and Enzo and the famous five all rush through the door, but Enzo lingers for a tiny second and sure enough, turns towards Jack, clapping his hands and holding his heart. 'Grazie,' he says, followed by a whole bucket-load of Italian that absolutely none of them can decipher in the slightest, but seems very earnest.

Later that night in his bunk above Jack's at the hostel, Silvio tries to recreate the words, given his loose Roman heritage, but his memory is shot and both of them are fighting sleep. And it's true, Jack still doesn't know what the little chap said, but he knows the makings of a good union. Had one himself for nearly thirty years. Doesn't want to talk about it.

'That there,' he will tell Silvio, as he drifts away in the cosy dryness. 'That there is a stayer.'

# VI. COUCH

IT IS IMPOSSIBLE to quantify how much truth there is to any story that comes out of Christie's gob, so from the age of ten, Elly stops trying. The simple facts are there, rendered in sepia: her mother as a leggy pin-up girl in perfect '60s attire, hanging off the arms of artists, club owners, Formula One drivers. There is the letter addressed to an as-yet unborn Elly from Charlie Watts, who scribbled it on the inside of an original pressing of *Some Girls*, presumably under the impression that this incoming daughter may actually be his. There's the paraphernalia, endless invitations, telegrams, backstage passes, first-class flight receipts. And of course, there are the articles, preserved behind plastic, telling the sorry tale of the small-town girl from Stockport who wound up rubbing shoulders with Bowie and Bolan before a dramatic car accident laid waste to her budding career as a model.

In every fading print, Christie is cackling, holding a wine glass and a cigarette, safe in the knowledge that these good times will last forever, that she will be eternally young and will never end up back in the woeful streets she shook off as a teenager, married to a perfectly nice chap and raising a somewhat misanthropic daughter. Gary, Elly's father, calls it the Strobe Light Complex. He says her mother was one of many women being hit by beams of light from the same source at around the same time, deluded into thinking they were singularly unique.

'Look, I won't deny your mother was an absolute knockout,' he says. 'But there were hundreds of girls like her in London back then. Nobody ate proper meals, everyone on uppers, smoking all the time. Drugs, abuse . . . it really was a disastrous time to be a young woman.'

Around the time of the accident, which is also around the time she puts a down payment on a purple velvet Chesterfield couch, having sat on one at a party thrown by Ginger Baker, Christie auditions for the Miss World competition. She is one of the top finalists from England and the ceremony, to be held at Royal Albert Hall, will be televised around the world, sure to make her an instant superstar. To hear Christie tell it, the organisers ring her to invite her to the semifinals at exactly the same moment she flies through the windscreen of her friend Grace's MG coupe, seatbelts not being the done thing in those days. Shards of glass sliced through her face and neck, embedding themselves inside tiny folds of her skin.

'My life started and ended in that instant,' she says, sprawled out on the same couch which she has provisionally loaned to her daughter. 'Hold on to your youth.'

Though Elly does not want any lasting reminders of her shattered family in her flat, even she has to admit that the Chesterfield is an excellent piece. Despite silently witnessing over half a century of heartbreak, it's held up remarkably well. Velvet, unlike Elly's mother, is a fabric that looks and feels better as it ages. Besides, it's kind of funny to have this loud emblem of the swinging '60s in a clean, minimalist flat, Elly thinks. It shows she isn't entirely predictable.

After her parents split up, Elly, as a precocious ten-year-old, decided they'd effectively lost rights to their godly titles. No longer able, in her eyes, to lay claim to the names 'Mum' and 'Dad', she instead relegated them to the names they had used before she was born (especially Christie, who she never called 'Mum' again) and started down the road that ended with them totally ruining her life.

Elly's plan is for Enzo never to meet Christie, at least not until he puts a ring on her finger and it's too late to back out. For the first year or two, it seems to work. They live in London, she is in Manchester, a city there is absolutely no reason to go to in her opinion, so they don't. Gary pops over on the way down to see cousins in Brighton, and the two men seem to get along well enough that he diverts his plans for the drive back so he can take Enzo to see the new Tarantino film with him at Picturehouse. It becomes a semi-regular thing, her boyfriend and her father pal-ing around doing man things, and she's not overly mad about it. But there is only so long she can deflect questions about Christie, especially after Enzo takes her back to Naples to meet all four generations of his family, from his nonna to his new nieces. She had thought that referring to Christie in the past tense might lead Enzo to believe she was dead, which in some ways would be preferable, but during one of their sporadic Thursday negroni sessions Gary lets slip that Elly's mother is very much alive and still Absolutely Fabulous, and after that it's all over.

Elly doesn't hate her mother so much as has extreme anxiety about her showing up unannounced, stamping around and shaking the foundations of anything pure and good in her life, something which has become a truism the older and more established she becomes. With age has arrived the understanding, something which barely registered as a glimmer when she was a child, that her mother resents having had her. The couch, which she loaned Elly with a very strict set of conditions when she first moved out of uni halls and into her own flat in East London – always spot clean, never spray with any hard chemical products, absolutely no animals under any circumstances – functions as something of a literal reminder of the good times Christie gave up to become a mother. Never mind that her career as a professional looker, if one could even call that a career, was dead on arrival after she torpedoed headfirst into the Marylebone end of Great Portland Street that fateful Wednesday afternoon. It was her child, the result of a brief and relatively clumsy shag with the very kind medical student who'd tended to her injuries and promptly fallen in love with her, who had sucked the oxygen out of her existence.

Enzo remains unaware of much of this salacious context, as his fiancée tends to avoid discussing Christie at all costs. He loves the purple couch, its texture and shimmer, and often spends much of his Saturday draped across it, bare feet up on the painted brick wall, one hand stroking Lola in a brazen act of defiance of Christie's rules, the other leafing through the pink pages of the *Financial Times Weekend.* In a flat full of mostly practical, muted furnishings, the couch represents to Enzo a more rock-and-roll side to his fiancée that simmers somewhere beneath her no-nonsense exterior, something wild and possibly even dangerous. He remains convinced of this unreality, because every time he asks after the couch's backstory – usually while reclining on it; he uses the thing far more than Elly, who still treats it with a certain level of wariness – Elly shuts down the conversation quickly. It remains the only piece of furniture they own that she will point blank refuse to fuck him on, no matter how many times he pleads.

Aware that the couch is special, it is where Enzo plans for Elly to be sitting when he eventually pops the question. After the Glastonbury incident and a subsequent month spent reviving his good nature through a combination of cognitive behavioural therapy and wild swimming, he is convinced more than ever that he owes any positivity in his life to her. His mother loves her. Sofia has already taken to calling her 'la sorella'. There is no further discussion required.

He knows that Elly hates diamonds – 'unsustainable, overdone and worthless the minute you walk them out of the shop' – but also that prior attempts to infuse her wardrobe with brighter tones have ended badly, so he settles halfway with a black diamond that he is absolutely ready to tell her is an opal if she asks, which she does not because she is too busy crying happy tears, blowing her nose and jumping up and down on the couch with her shoes on while calling everyone she knows, except, of course, her mother.

Enzo is understandably thrilled, then, to discover Elly has recently acquiesced, inviting her mother over for tea to celebrate the news of their engagement. Heading Hackney way is a serious commitment for a woman like Christie, who spent many years completely oblivious to the idea that there was anything to London beyond the lopsided periphery of Seven Dials, Carnaby Street and Golden Square. Whenever she returns to the city that both made and broke her, Christie maintains the illusion that it is still at the tail end of its greatest era and she is still nineteen, flush with some poor mug's cash and living it up in Soho. Even pushing seventy, she's still in remarkably good nick, sashaying about Liberty dragging bunches of expensive dresses in cuts and sizes long outlawed for women of her age. It's not the same in Manchester, where she is onto her fourth or fifth post-divorce boyfriend; life is much slower, duller and the people are kind, lacking in edge or bite. They know what it means to work hard, something one could never accuse Christie of, and to put food on the table. So it is not unusual for Elly's mother to be drunk on life (and, more than she would care to admit, on Campari) whenever she alights at Leicester Square.

All of this information has been deliberately withheld from Enzo for so long that Elly now believes it impossible to prepare him adequately and safely for the imminent arrival of Cyclone

Christie, something she herself only decided to green-light some forty-eight hours ago. She feels this may be the disaster that unravels the first proper relationship she's had since Lily Allen was discovered on Myspace, and is dreadfully nervous, unable to sleep or eat in the lead-up to Sunday afternoon. Enzo, who has never met a mother he couldn't charm the Spanx off, finds her anxiety slightly overwrought, until the morning of the day Christie is due to arrive, when Elly finally lands on the cultural reference to help explain the septuagenarian teenager that is her biological mother.

'You know the film *Austin Powers*?' she asks him as they order double espressos at the counter of a plant store down Lower Clapton Road that doubles as a cafe, because of course it does.

'Si, Mike Myers. So funny. I watch so many times. Second one is my favourite. "*Yeah baby, yeah.*"'

'Right. Do you remember why he was so funny, though?'

'Bad teeth?' Enzo offers, doing the twist. 'Silly dancing?'

'No,' she snaps, as they weave their way through mazes of 60-quid monsteras in 40-pound pots, perspiring under the conservatory's micro-climate. Finally, she spots a free table and Enzo lunges for it.

'It's that he's from the wrong time,' she says, downing the rest of her coffee. 'He's rolling around in the '90s dressed like a swinger with his floral shirts and blue velvet suits. It's fucking ridiculous. He's an anachronism, that's where the gag is. The guy wakes up from a cryogenic sleep and just acts like nothing has changed.'

'Babe, I – you know I don't know these words.'

'Sorry, Darling. What I'm trying to say is that Austin Powers can't get it into his head that it isn't the era of free love anymore. And what's worse is that everyone else indulges him, so he gets to tear about London, dressed like a muppet, saying things like "totally shagadelic baby" as if feminism never happened.'

'I don't understand,' says Enzo, flipping his empty cup back and forth. 'Is film. Make-up things. Austin Powers, un personaggio fittizio.'

'Yes of course. I know he isn't real. But unfortunately, my mother is – and she's exactly the same.'

While the windscreen looms large in the retelling of the Christie myth, the truth is she actually went through two panes of glass, not one. Jittery with diet pills, Grace's lead foot landed so hard on the brakes that Christie soared well clear of the MG, flying over its nose and smashing into the shop window of a local haberdashery, where she landed rather ingloriously on a pile of groovy, bell-bottom suits that wouldn't have looked out of place in *Austin Powers*. Her face, neck and shoulders were pocked with so many tiny shards of glass that she practically glinted under the harsh hospital lights. Unable to afford an extended convalescence in Harley Street Hospital, which happened to be mere streets away from her final touchdown, she instead opted to return to Stockport, ra-ra skirts in her trunk and tail firmly between her legs, the only of her defining features to escape the accident unscathed.

Fresh out of medical school and still brimming with the ambition and promise that eventually evaporates in all doctors, Gary was on the ward the night Christie the human mirror ball was admitted. He'd never encountered a woman quite like her; lighting a continuous stream of fags in her room despite his registrar's protestations, refusing to eat anything that wasn't liquefied, strained or pulped for fear of going up a size during her recuperation, and playing her collection of rock-and-roll 45s on her portable Penny record player, which she'd somehow convinced the paramedics to grab from her basement flat before her hasty evacuation from the big smoke. In the '90s, they would write TV comedies centred around women like Christie, but if you ask Gary – and Elly did, especially after the divorce – they never quite captured her fizzy, manic energy. Everything Christie touched turned to sequins and Gary, along with practically every red-blooded male in the hospital, was infuriatingly, stupidly in love with her. The oath he had taken upon becoming a doctor meant Gary had to wait six long months – the time it took for Christie to walk confidently again and for the surgeons to remove the final slivers from around her cat's eyes, one blue, one green, and discharge her – to phone her at her parents' house and ask if she might like to go for dinner.

In Gary's favour, had you asked Christie – which Elly never did, but she frequently told her anyway – were his good looks, amiable disposition, empathy and noted distaste for the high life. Moreover, two days back at home was enough to make Christie want to attempt to better her own record and launch through three sheets of glass, hell, five even, if it meant never having to hear her father read the classifieds out loud, job listings for secretaries or phone switchboard operators or the typing pool, as if the best possible outcome for a woman of her vivacity was to give up on life like everyone else in Stockport. Gary, with his goofy smile, solid job and kind temperament was Christie's ticket out – or so she thought. Within a year they were hitched and, at Christie's insistence, relocated back to London and to Soho, where she resumed an only slightly less debauched version of her past life, one that pickled her liver, wore out the enamel of her original teeth and would have undeniably killed her marriage dead at a far earlier juncture were it not for the arrival of a sudden queasiness during an uncharacteristic spell off the sauce, a weird, clammy seasickness that she had always attributed to vodka without having eaten lunch, but which in fact signalled, she realised with great dismay, that despite every effort to lacerate herself internally, at the somewhat prime age of thirty-one, the worst had finally happened. Christie, the sequin sorceress of Soho, was pregnant.

Elly buys three too many boxes of crackers, more cheese than fits in the fridge. She frets about the cutlery, of all things.

'The nice set is stained,' she shouts, holding up a gold teaspoon, 'and the regular stuff looks cheap!'

This frenzy to Elly seems entirely justified; she has to impress upon her mother that she is living well despite not living to excess – something for which Christie has always berated her – while also providing a neutral daytime environment in which there is no valid reason to consume alcohol. Their entire household stash has been squirrelled away into old moving boxes upstairs in the loft or behind thick winter coats in the bedroom wardrobe. Elly has entrusted the good stuff – Enzo's superior collection of liqueurs and a few posh bottles of red – to Oli, who promises not to indulge in exchange for at least two free pizzas.

'Explain to me,' Enzo says, after they bury the last of the contraband from view. 'She is alcoholic?'

'Alcoholics have a problem with drinking. Christie has a love affair with it.'

'Si, okay. But if she drinks a lot and you worry about it, is hiding a good idea?'

They sat together at the edge of the loft, dangling their legs over the floor below. It was one of their favourite places to talk openly, because they didn't have to look at each another.

'I don't follow,' she says.

'My Uncle Fausto. You met him, when we went to Napoli. With the big moustache?'

Elly mentally runs through the 52-card set of Enzo's extended family, searching for the right face.

'Oh yes. He was very funny. Really good at English, too.'

Enzo stares at the arched windows. His pancaked thighs show the makings of a nervous tremor.

'So he was drunk. Drunk whole weekend.'

'He was?'

'About ten years ago, maybe twenty, my papa and his papa, they do, when you get involved in someone's problems . . .'

'An intervention?'

'Si, and it go nowhere. Fausto is angry all the time. He get very physical with Donna. So bad that one day, they decide, just let him drink, you know? Easier for everyone in the family.'

'Why have you never told me this before?'

'Is not important,' he says. 'Also, you never tell me about your mama. Never.'

Elly considers this for a moment.

'Well, it doesn't matter anyway. Christie's not like that. She's a fucking tornado, but when she's pissed, she's like an atomic bomb. Nobody survives.'

'Maybe I can –'

'It might make her happier, but it'll make our lives so much worse. So no; cheese, crackers, tea and Hobnobs, thank you and good night.'

In addition to wooing mothers, one of Enzo's other untold skills is knowing exactly when an argument is about to enter a death spiral. He nuzzles up to Elly's neck and kisses behind her ear, a guaranteed reset.

'She's your mama. She loves you. Everything will be fine.'

Realising that they'd be unable to raise a family on a junior doctor or senior socialite's salary, Gary and Christie boxed up their flat and returned again to the dreariness of Stockport, only to discover that in the intervening years, Manchester had undergone something of a renaissance. While still largely a working-class, red-brick town, the arrival of the '80s had brought with it an explosive new scene, taking in Factory Records, all-night raves and the storied rise of Hacienda. There were bold new outfits and even better drugs, but Christie, already cresting forty in her imagination and miserably stuck inside raising a fussy, crying toddler, was going to have to sit this one out.

Instead, Elly would be reared on a diet of anthems – 'Blue Monday', 'Kinky Afro', 'Bizarre Love Triangle', 'Fool's Gold' – that her mother could only order from the Piccadilly Records catalogue, instead of writhing along to in – or on – ecstasy at the club. To be outside looking in on a happening cultural moment was something of a spiritual death for Christie, who attempted to rejoin the party when her daughter was old enough to be left with dotty Mrs Mendick downstairs, but found that her moves were all wrong, the clothes were all angular and unflattering and despite her inherent enthusiasm for experimentation, ecstasy did not agree with her at all.

Quietly cowed, she slunk back to her husband, who had inexplicably become a top doctor with his own practice despite raising what often seemed like two young children, and promptly renewed her relationship with gin, which did not judge her for being mutton dressed as lamb, or snicker at her in the queue at midnight. It was always 1968 when Christie drank; her legs were taut and her tits were magnificent. There were no grubby, precocious little brats that always needed something, asking maths questions that Christie hadn't even known the answers to the first time around. This lifestyle choice proved something of a conundrum for Gary, who was getting used to coming home from the surgery to discover his wife passed out on the settee by 5 pm, Elly balanced precariously on the chair trying to reach the pack of McVities on the shelf, having once again been left to her own devices when it came to supper. Once she started boozing again, Christie tended to play her music loud, and Gary could usually hear one of the three Ians – Dury, Brown, or Curtis if it was a bad day – blaring from down the street.

But even when she was a ghastly beast of a woman, Gary loved her with an ardour that bordered on fanatical and, emulating his own parents, who had stayed together for over fifty years despite their fair share of troubles, he endured. Even when inebriated, Christie remained utterly alluring, charming even. The dark side of her drunkenness that aligned with meanness was one rarely chanced upon by Gary, more frequently reserved for her knock-kneed daughter. And so, when she finally upped and left around the time Elly had finished primary school, the real mystery to many of their friends and family was why Gary hadn't walked first. That is, to everyone but Elly, who realised almost immediately that her mother wasn't separating from her father, but from her.

So fixated is she upon micromanaging every last detail around Christie's arrival, Elly neglects to recall the most important of them all, which is that she lives directly across the street from a well-known pub. The error of her ways is revealed almost as soon as she opens the door, where she is greeted by a reeking blast so pungent that it almost seems like the spirits Christie has imbibed secretly have become an actual spirit and are now using her body as a host. Emboldened with enough Dutch courage that she could easily command their navy, Christie storms straight past Elly, through the fading afternoon light and into the expectant embrace of her future son-in-law.

'Well, aren't you a handsome little thing,' she coos, standing back and gripping Enzo's shoulders like he's a little boy and she's trying to see how much he's grown. 'In the '70s, I used to eat men like you alive.'

The toxic waft of booze catches up with her and slithers up Enzo's nose. His olfactory processor detects more than just the clear stuff; there are also top notes of house white and rosé and somewhere beneath the solid middle of gin, what smells like the remnants of a shandy. He wonders how long Christie has been holding court at The Pembury. It seems like the entire weekend.

Christie exclaims, and Enzo assumes it's at the striking vision of her daughter, having gone to the effort to wear a significant amount of pink for her benefit. But rather, the object of her affections is her beloved purple couch that she's spied in the corner. She throws herself upon it, stroking the fabric with her lacquered nails and sighing like a long-lost lover.

'Eloise,' she calls, acknowledging her own daughter for the first time since she arrived, 'fix me a drink, won't you? Campari, rocks. You'll have some of that with an Italian in the house, no doubt.'

Christie totters a bit, hands gripping the velvet, trying to hold it together. 'I mean, we just have to have a toast, dear. We must. This is a *celebration*, isn't it?'

It's not clear whether she's talking to Elly or simply to herself.

It's getting dark. Christie has returned to The Pembury less than an hour after she left, her seat by the bar still warm. Recriminations hover above the untouched cheese and crackers. Elly slumps forward on the velvet couch, black mascara running past her black diamond ring that her mother didn't even ask to see. Having been shrugged off a number of times already, Enzo perches on the armrest, contemplating what to do next.

She dabs her eyes with a Kleenex. 'Well, that's that. We never have to see her again.'

Enzo is somewhat taken aback. 'Never?'

'Were we just in the same room? She's a complete fucking disaster. And even worse than that, she's mean. I've spent years trying to get out from under her. *Years*. I don't know why I ever thought this was a good idea. But you needed to see it for yourself, because now you get what I'm on about.'

'Babe,' he says deliberately, trying to find the right phrasing, 'she is mental and very, very loud, but she is still your mama.'

'This bullshit about family, Enzo, I don't want to hear it,' she says, voice flat. 'I'm thrilled you all love each other, really, but that's not how it works in the real world. This is what it looks like. Disappointment after disappointment. Having to make time for that witch just because she decided not to abort me. You know, sometimes I wish she bloody had.'

She surveys herself, plainly disgusted to have compromised on her usual outfit to impress a mother who cannot be pleased. The bright colours feel venomous, like they are bleeding into her skin. Elly barely recognises herself. In a sudden fit of rage, she bolts into the kitchen, tears everything off and dumps it in the bin, stomping back to the open living room in her bra and knickers.

Enzo doesn't know what to say. This is a new development for him, which a small voice inside his head says may be the basis of a much larger problem. Eventually he finds what he believes to be the correct response.

'Okay.' He slides down next to her. 'Si, family is everything. But you are my family now. And you are not your mama. You will be different; you will be better.'

Elly leans against him, sniffling. Unlike their radiators, Enzo can always be relied upon to be warm.

'You have too much faith in me, Darling. I love you so much, but sometimes I think you're as crazy as she is.'

'Is possible,' he smiles. 'We both love this couch.'

And just like that, Elly has an idea. A sweet piece of vengeance, against herself and Christie. A clear separation of the past and her bright new future.

It's not that much of a stretch, really.

She's practically naked already.

**Patrick Smith-Jones 09.10**
**Hi, is this still available?**

Patrick said he wouldn't be picking up the couch personally on account of his being seventy-eight years old, but that he'd like to drop by and inspect it before he sent some strapping young boys over to carefully transport it back to his place in Chelsea. His rapid responsiveness and overall proficiency with Marketplace's messaging interface was surprising. Unlike Jane, he seemed to have few quibbles with technology, save for using LOL in the wrong context, and appeared to be online day and night. In a recent briefing session for designing a new retirement complex that we'd had at work, I'd heard about a trend in older people using apps to feel less lonely, but Patrick didn't strike me as someone whiling away his remaining days trying to find a friend. Rather, by his own admission, Patrick was Quite Wonderful and didn't feel a day over forty – though his sciatica and niggling left knee begged to differ.

Patrick 00.34
Am 1 foot into the grave as they say but honestly, never felt quite so alive.

Patrick 00.46
speaking of which I've been hunting 4 a chesterfield in this colour longer than you've been on this earth!

Elly 00.52
don't you know it's rude to ask a woman
how old she is

Patrick 01.12
of course please 4give me. I wouldn't want
to be ageist 😉

On a hunch, I searched Patrick's full name between our rapid-fire online banter. There were more than sixteen pages of results. It was hard to get a clear picture of what exactly Patrick's line of work had once been, but multiple features from *Forbes* and *The Robb Report* indicated that he was now perhaps most well-known – aside from being a significant patron of English theatre – for how he spent his money.

Patrick 09.30
i'm what u would call a collector.

Elly 09.33
like stamps and old pennies?

Patrick 09.38
u laugh but I once sold a single stamp for £4000.

*Vogue* had commissioned two separate photo shoots of Patrick's house in the space of a decade, detailing his incredible array of period furniture that stretched across eras and continents.

He'd been the subject of a *Wallpaper* cover story and gushingly profiled in *Monocle*, discussing the value of investing in quality design; the article also noted that George Michael had tried unsuccessfully to shoot a music video in his house on a number of occasions.

All of this made me think briefly about whether my asking price for the couch was too low. Patrick seemed to be the kind of discerning man who knew exactly how much things were worth, and it was very possible that the £1500 price tag I'd tacked onto the old sofa had transformed it into a huge bargain. It could be worth loads, I heard Sensible Me chide in the back of my head. He's clearly a multimillionaire, maybe even a billionaire. You're just going to give it to him for pocket change? He probably drops this much on champagne or caviar every other week.

Yes, I thought to myself, while liaising with Patrick for the third day straight to finally arrange a time for him to come by and check the couch out, that's precisely what I'm going to do. I just want the damn thing gone.

'*My*,' Patrick said, surveying the almost-bare living room. 'I've read about Marie Kondo, but this really is something else.'

'Yes, well, it's not really tidying so much as offloading,' I replied.

'Honestly, dear? I'm worried that if I take this lounge, there won't be anything left.'

'That's kind of the point.'

'So the plan is to divest yourself of all your earthly possessions and, what? Achieve some form of inner peace?'

'More about cleansing the place of demons, if you get me.'

'Demons or ghosts? They can be quite different, you know.'

'Whatever they are, you buy the couch, mate, you can have them for free.'

Patrick fixed his chestnut-brown eyes on me before launching into what seemed like a well-oiled mission statement. He walked loping circles around the empty room as he talked, unimpeded by the large table and chairs I no longer owned.

'Before we proceed any further, I need you to understand that I make it my business to know the full story behind any piece I purchase. Vintage furniture has its own aura, you know. If something is off, it doesn't matter how you position it or which room you place it in; it never quite works. Bad juju can infect an entire space instantaneously. You can't just feng shui your way out of it. And that can be quite frustrating when you've spent a fair bit of money.'

'I'll give you an example,' he continued. 'A few years ago, I bought this absolutely exquisite antique drinks cabinet. Made in the 1940s in Budapest, solid walnut. The detailing on it, you would just absolutely die. Nobody makes them like that anymore. Only three of its kind left in the entire world; the Germans got to the rest and used them for kindling. So, I finally found it at an auction after a very lengthy search and had it shipped back to my house, but for some reason it felt as if it didn't really fit anywhere. I think I had it moved a hundred times. Tried it every which way. Eventually, I called the auction house and asked them to issue a provenance report, whereupon I discovered that it had originally belonged to a pair of clandestine Hungarian homosexuals, who were rounded up with all the other undesirables by the SS and sent to the camps to perish. And now this cursed thing sat in my house! No, I simply cannot abide evil energy like that. It ruins everything.'

'Do you still have it, the cabinet?' I asked.

'Oh, lord no. I sold it right back to them at a tidy profit and then donated the lot to Stonewall.'

We both laughed.

'Well listen, let me put your mind at ease,' I said. 'No Nazis were involved in my procurement of this couch. I'm almost certain it's a post-war piece.'

Patrick walked over to the couch to conduct an initial survey, before easing himself slowly down onto it. He traced two fingers along one of its curled arms.

'I should say so. The report I received said it's a late '60s original.'

'How do you commission a report on something you haven't seen in real life?'

Teasingly, he put a blistered finger to his lips. 'There are in this country a great many people whose peculiar skills do not translate to traditional vocations. Take Julian, who has worked for me for a good twenty years. From a single, low-quality photograph, he can ascertain the year, make, model and authenticity of practically any piece of furniture made since 1600. Left school at fifteen, but his knowledge is invaluable.'

'Must be nice to be able to afford your own personal search engine.'

'Oh, it is very nice, yes,' he said. 'But more than that, it's essential. Imagine how much time I'd waste going round to young girls' houses like yours, only to find out down the line that their classic Eames chairs were shoddy replicas.'

'And now that you've done your due diligence, how significantly have I fucked myself over with this asking price?'

Patrick grinned with a face full of teeth that definitely weren't the ones he was born with. Deeply etched smile lines arced up from the corners of his mouth, connecting seamlessly with the crows' feet near his eyes.

'You should know by now that a gentleman never tells.'

It wasn't long after this that Patrick asked politely for wine, a little glass of white if I had any half-decent in the chiller, which was an inspired request as booze was generally the only thing in my fridge these days aside from single-serve yoghurt pots and three-day old chorizo pizza from The Pembury. I stuck my head inside the positively arctic Smeg and realised that I'd forgotten to replenish my stash and the only thing I had left to offer was the dregs of a bottle of Bombay – without any tonic.

'Purple Chesterfield, three-seater, 1969, Baum Brothers . . .' he called to me as I rummaged through the crisper, past a crumpled avocado that looked as though it may already have begun mutating.

'. . . those are the facts, sure, but they're not the *story*. How did this item come into your possession, almost fifty years after the fact? Who did it pass through to get to you? That's what fascinates me. It's why I'm here, on the other side of London, on a Monday. I want to hear it all, from the very beginning.'

I ducked my head out the door to take another look at him, rocking back and forth on the couch, eyes closed as if in a dream. Everything about Patrick was precise, from the pleats in his trousers to the folds in the green silk cravat he wore around his throat. Silver rings adorned almost all of his fingers, punctuated by emerald, ruby and sapphire. It was the sort of look that, on someone my age, would come off as utterly disingenuous; a fuckboy trying to be Johnny Depp trying to be a pirate. But Patrick carried it off as if he'd invented it. I'd never met my grandparents, who had all died just after I was born, but in that instant, I'd never wanted one more.

'I'm really sorry about this,' I said, slamming the fridge shut. 'I just wasn't expecting to host today so there's nothing in the –'

There was a polite rap at the door. I looked over at Patrick, who shrugged mischievously like some kind of schoolboy.

The security gate swung open to reveal a stern-faced man in a freshly pressed grey suit. He presented me two bottles of sauv blanc that I'd later discover were worth a few hundred quid each and couldn't be found at any old off-licence. 'For Master Patrick, and yourself of course,' he said, before promptly disappearing down the lane past Chicken Shop Run.

'How many goons do you have hiding out there?' I asked as I came back inside.

'Not as many as I have enemies.'

'Do they carry fancy wine for protection? Am I holding lethal weapons?'

'Hardly, dear. If you're going to maul some aggrieved chap with a broken bottle, always make sure to use the cheap stuff.'

'You didn't answer my question. Anyway, I take it that was Julian.'

'Yes, he's quite a mysterious fellow,' Patrick said, signalling towards the cupboard where he correctly presumed my wine glasses were kept. 'I always try to have him around, especially when embarking on dangerous safaris through the East End.'

I held up the bottles. Patrick nodded towards the one in my right hand.

As I brought the wine over, it occurred to me that my scarcity of stuff was becoming an issue for future guests I didn't want. The couch was now it as far as furniture went; there was nothing else left in the room on which to perch. I handed Patrick his glass and sat down on the floor opposite. I was getting very used to the floor. My bum didn't even fall asleep anymore.

'Look, there's not much by way of a story. Christie – sorry, Mum – said she bought the couch from someone who played in Cream. Or maybe it was Hendrix's bass player, the white guy with the big hair? I can't remember the details. I don't really care, anyway. She probably just got it from a catalogue, but there's no mythology around catalogues, is there?'

'Sounds to me like she got up to a fair bit of mischief.'

'That's putting it politely.'

'Wonder if I knew her. One imagines we're not that far apart in age.'

'Pretty sure she'd argue the toss on that.'

'Ah yes, one of *those.*'

'I don't know, were you hanging around lots of leggy blondes with serious drinking problems in the late '60s?'

'Almost exclusively, dear. Everyone had a drinking problem back then. We called it "Monday".'

'Well, this Monday's gone on for half a century. Getting a bit long now.'

'I see,' he said, patting the couch. 'But how exactly did it get here? To this flat?'

'Surely Julian's already found that out by sniffing my old knickers or rummaging through my mail out there?'

'My dear, you have a lot to learn about decorum – and this is coming from someone who discovered he was gay the same year as Elton John.'

'I didn't know there were homosexuals in the Jurassic era.'

Patrick harumphed, wheezing as he choked on wine that had gone down the wrong way.

'That was good, Elly. I'll let you have that one for free.'

I felt the beginning of what I imagined was a genuine grin creep onto my face. It was an extremely foreign sensation; one I knew was unlikely to last.

'You're too kind. Now, what were you asking again? Oh yes, how it got here. On a truck, from Hoxton. Before that, on another truck, from Manchester. But it was bought – or stolen – in London somewhere first, so basically, it's been ferried up and down the M1 for about forty or fifty years.'

'It must be quite something to have been kept in your family for all this time. And now you're flogging it.'

'I've recently disposed of a partner, so the cash is more important. This place doesn't pay for itself. Also, the damn thing reminds me more of him than it does her, for some strange reason. Bad juju, like you said.'

He paused. 'Long-term?'

I flashed my left hand at him. I'd taken to wearing the ring again, as some sort of maudlin talismanic ritual. I hadn't had my nails done in ages, and it killed me how good it still looked.

'Oh dear,' he said. 'Well, go on then. Paint me a picture since I can't see any around here.'

'Do you know Jamie Cullum, the musician?'

'I think I do, yes. He was on Jools recently. Short chap. Very lively. Dances on his piano a lot.'

'That's the one. Now just give him stronger facial hair and a Neapolitan accent.'

'Oh, an Italian!' he exclaimed. 'I adore Italian men. So classically handsome . . .'

'Yes, well. As did I. But he's gone now and I . . .'

'. . . need to part ways with your mother's lounge?'

'With due respect to the almighty couch, I'm selling almost everything.'

'It's a piece of your history, though, isn't it?'

'You know, that's funny,' I said. 'Christie calls it a family heirloom.'

'She's right, actually. An heirloom doesn't have to be jewellery, or a special piece of clothing. Really, it's anything with emotional or financial value passed down through generations.'

I stared at Patrick.

'Don't be daft. An heirloom is worth something. This is just a relic, a marker of some other time. Bit like my mum, frankly.'

'You really don't like her, do you?'

'Call it a defensive position. She'd prefer it if I'd never been born.'

'I'm sorry, she *said* that to you?'

Weirdly electrified by how much this seemed to affect the old man, I pressed on.

'I'll put it another way: if this whole flat was on fire – like serious film shit, stuff melting, flames up the walls – and she had to choose between saving that couch or me, you'd find her passed out from smoke inhalation trying to push it through the door.'

Patrick sighed and stared out the window as he cracked his knuckles. He embodied the sort of easy assuredness that, Enzo had explained to me over the years, naturally affixed itself to the postures of the super-rich.

'If you want to know a man is worth hundred, maybe two hundred million pounds,' he'd said, 'you look at their neck. They never sit straight, is a sign of being interested. Giveaway. But neck is always moving. All big money have strong neck. Neck is connected to head, like CCTV. So they seem relaxed, but they always watching. They survey everything.'

I'd asked him if rich women, like the Princess of Monaco, or Kim Kardashian, had the same behavioural tics.

'No, is very different,' he'd said with some gravity. 'Rich women know is always a man trying to take their millions. They like this –' he sat ramrod straight like a kid trying to avoid detention, 'all the time. Think; you never see Elizabeth Holmes hunch. She looks like there is steel beam straight up from her culo to her brain.'

Enzo could reel off the key stats around bonza rich people the way football tragics did with league fixtures. But it didn't mean he particularly enjoyed his main line of work, which from what I had gathered over the years mostly entailed writing portfolio summaries hidden behind a corporate paywall that the majority of people never even got to read.

In an effort to future-proof himself against writing bullet-point blog posts for the rest of his life, he'd accepted a left-field offer of some freelance work for the luxury magazine of the *Financial Times*. Enzo's ease and familiarity with the staggeringly well-off afforded him a relatively painless entrée to some of the most fiercely contested column inches in the country – paid handsomely, issued sparsely, and read fawningly by some of the worst people ever born. The only good thing about it was the title – *How To Spend It.* I thought it was absolutely fucking brilliant. Enzo didn't see the joke.

'It's a double meaning.'

'Sorry Babe, I no follow.'

'*How To Spend It.*'

'"You rich, here is how to spend your money."'

'Yes, that's the first layer, but there's more to it.'

'No there isn't. Is glossy magazine for millionaires.'

'That's exactly it. Do you remember how you told me sometimes the British say one thing but mean something different?'

'Si, like when they say "Alright" but they not actually asking if you actually alright. So annoying!'

'Right, well *How To Spend It* is like that. Imagine you came to my house, and I offered to make you a coffee. Now, you're Italian, so obviously you know how to make it properly. You come over to the machine and you say "Hey, Elly. Don't worry, I'll show you *how to make coffee*."'

Enzo's eyes widened.

'It's not just a guide. It's a judgement. *How To Spend It* says "Sure, you just made a billion taking your app public, but what are you going to do with all that dosh? You have no taste." It congratulates you and embarrasses you in the same sentence. Kind of amazing, actually.'

'But Babe, this is *mean*, no?'

'Not really, Darling. It's just English.'

'I appreciate that this is going to sound strange,' Patrick said, bringing me back into the room, 'but I have to ask: this former flame of yours, what does he do for a living?'

'He's in financial services journalism.'

'So business, markets, that sort of thing?'

'Mostly he profiles high-net-worth individuals. He interviews them and writes these little summary sheets other millionaires like you subscribe to, so you can make sure your superyacht is still bigger.'

'Fascinating,' Patrick said. 'I imagine he must have put in some hours with our nation's nouveau riche.'

'Yes, the *How To Spend It* crowd. "Here's your guide to how to buy something disgustingly expensive, instead of just expensively disgusting."'

Patrick chuckled.

'You know, the editors of that publication like to call on me every so often for this and that. Offer up some guidance, I suppose, as to how those inheritance-tax dodgers and start-up pricks should most effectively squander their billions.'

'Like what?' I guffawed. 'Which is the best diamond-encrusted Rolex to pair with a lime-green Lamborghini?'

'Anyway,' he continued unflappably, slugging the rest of his wine and refilling both our glasses, 'I do have something of a reputation for disbursing my wealth without being overly ostentatious about it, which I believe endears me to that lot. One day Hugh, who is the features man over there, calls me while I'm holidaying in Mustique – as I tend to do when the winter starts to nip at the toes – and asks if I wouldn't mind holding court for a dashing young journalist who asks good questions and knows exactly where the line is. Now, I've never said no to entertaining handsome members of the press, though I do recall this fellow wasn't exactly part of the establishment. He seemed to be trying it out for size . . .'

I wasn't sure I liked where this story was going and tried to give Patrick the kind of withering stare that was universally understood as 'drop it'. It appeared the old man hadn't picked up social cues as fast as he had internet slang.

'About two weeks later this most gorgeous specimen arrives at my gate with his shiny black dictaphone and we just talk for ages. A natural conversationalist, I remember thinking, which is what separates the good interviewers from the highly annoying ones. He must have left at some obscene hour, close to half-one in the morning. I believe the piece was all about how to purchase your first sculpture directly from the artist, which anyone can do, really, but all the examples they used started at a few million pounds. Separate the wheat from the chaff, as it were. So, there I am, chatting to this fellow about Kapoors and Kusamas and he's not really interested in how much they cost, or how difficult they are to acquire, but how they make me *feel*. Can you imagine? And I thought to myself, well this is something you don't hear every day. It ended up being a bit of a therapy session for both of us, none of which made it into the piece, of course, but I always wondered about him and where he'd landed in life. And you know, Elly, it wasn't until you told me your ex-husband was an Italian journalist that it occurred to me that we may, in fact, be referring to the same person, in which case I offer my most heartfelt sympathies because he really was a fantastic little man.'

He slumped back onto the couch, exhausted, like he'd just survived choking on something awful. I stared at a dirty spot on the wooden floor, trying to process this unlikely barrage of information.

It took me a few minutes to break the terse silence that had filled the flat.

'That was too good. Almost seemed pre-rehearsed. I'll have you know you're not getting the couch any cheaper.'

'Cross my heart,' he said, 'I tell no lies.'

'Besides, it's definitely just a coincidence. There must be loads of other Italian journalists in the UK.'

'Surely. Shall I call Julian in? Perhaps he can find the article archived on his phone.'

'No, you know what? It doesn't matter.'

Patrick held out his bony hand, pulling me up onto the couch.

'Elly,' he offered sagely as I sat down next to him. 'A piece of advice. You're too young to hate both your mother and your partner already. Save that for when you get closer to my age.'

'I . . . I don't hate him. But I thought it would be better by now and instead it's like this fucking splinter in my cuticle that keeps pushing deeper and deeper into my skin.'

'And you really think ridding yourself of all your earthly possessions, like this couch neither of you even bought, is going to help you extract it?'

'Short of shaving all my hair off or joining the military, it's probably my best bet.'

Patrick placed his glass on the windowsill. 'When did you last speak with him?'

'I haven't.'

'Not once?'

'No. Nothing from him, either.'

'When?'

'Summer. Over six months ago.'

Patrick whistled softly through his very obvious veneers. 'But he must have left some of his things, surely.'

'Oh yes, a wardrobe full of shirts and chinos, a rack of winter coats and two different pasta makers.'

'And he never even asked for any of it? How strange.'

'Maybe it's easier to buy a whole new life than fix the old one? Who knows.'

'I hate to say it, but the old adage goes that if they don't come running back, they typically don't come back at all.'

'Who said that?'

'I did. It's an adage and I'm old.'

I laughed.

'You're wonderful, Patrick. I can see why he'd want to chat with you all evening.'

'Assuming it is *him* we're talking about. As we've established, there's an overflowing diaspora of Italian finance journalists.'

'Probably better not to know. It'll hardly make a difference now.'

'Maybe not to you. But I did say I wanted the real story of the Chesterfield, and your story? This is it. It's a love story. Your mother's really just a bit player in this production.'

'When you said you were a collector,' I said to Patrick, exasperated, 'did you mean of other people's miseries?'

'Of course,' he cackled. 'Happy endings are for cartoons.'

*

With that, Patrick magicked his phone from his waistcoat and tapped it a few times to summon Julian, presumably from beneath one of the train station arches that shot out from behind the east wing of the building. This no-nonsense approach was something I'd always admired about the grey generation; they always seemed to know exactly when a conversation was over. Reflexively, I found myself bouncing out of the couch, as if to somehow make out like this sudden wrap-up had been my idea.

'So, er, yeah. Cool. How do you want to do this?'

'Julian will come and appraise the piece personally, though I don't foresee any issues. I'll send some removalists I trust tomorrow evening, if that's alright with you. Unless . . .'

'Don't worry,' I said, a little too abruptly, 'I've clearly nowhere to be.'

'Now, about that. I host a little salon of sorts at my townhouse in Marylebone a few times a year, where all the interesting characters I've met get to meet one another . . .'

I picked up the glasses and the empty bottle and headed over to the sink.

'You want me to hang at some soirée of the rich and famous? I've just about missed my second month of rent. Everything in my fridge has gone rank. Can't imagine I'll be very good company.'

Julian rapped politely at the door, which I opened with the casual laissez-faire of someone who had known him his entire life.

'That's why I prefer playing host,' Patrick continued. 'The only judge of character is me.'

'These the original cushions?' Julian asked, crouching down by the couch's base.

Now that I was paying proper attention, his voice was higher than expected and very clearly from somewhere near Newcastle.

'How would I know? I'm meant to be offloading a couch, not shooting an episode of *Antiques Roadshow* in my bloody house.'

'Elly here has recently been through a very serious break-up,' Patrick offered by way of explanation for my outburst.

'Aye, the worst. Tell us where he lives; Pat and I can go run him over in the Rolls. Nothing quite like having your legs crushed by a £300,000 car.'

'An appraiser and an enforcer,' I said to Patrick. 'Nice.'

'I did say he was a man of many talents.'

Julian stood up and brushed himself off.

'All kosher, boss. Original legs, velvet in top condition given the vintage. Seal on the underside confirms the date of production as '69.'

'Fab,' I said. 'Now, is Julian the money man too?'

Nobody said anything, so I ploughed on.

'It's just, if you could sort the cash out now, given we all agree it is what I said it is, that would really help me out with my landlord situation . . .'

Patrick and Julian looked at each other and burst out in hysterics. It took a while for them to calm down enough to speak.

'Sorry love,' Julian said. ''Fraid you've got the wrong end of the stick there. We don't carry that kind of money in cash. That's just mad.'

'I was hoping to send you the payment via bank transfer,' Patrick added.

'When, though? I know this is amusing to you, but I could be evicted here. Lex is a sweetheart, but he's got every right to throw me out on my arse.'

'Julian will take down your information and send it tonight,' Patrick said, his voice edging towards businesslike as he peeled himself slowly off the couch.

'Alright, alright. Sound. As long as this isn't some sort of vaudeville double-act you lot have going on, where you prey on young girls to rinse them of their stuff. I mean, how is it that you don't have a few hundred quid stashed in the glovebox of your third Ferrari or whatever you drove over here in? Isn't that the entire bloody point of being a millionaire?'

Patrick stopped in the middle of the empty square that had once been our living room.

'Ferrari. *Ferrari.* That was it.'

'What was?'

'The chap I did the interview with. I remember his name now. Enzo. Like Enzo Ferrari. We had a long discussion about it.'

I was not going to cry. I needed this cash, more than anything. £1500 would keep me going until next month when I went to stay with Gary and then I'd figure it out. Besides, I was so close to getting rid of it all. I was not going to cry. No weakness. Get them out the door, get the money, get on with it.

'There you have it,' I said eventually, trying so hard to keep my voice level that I could feel every muscle in my neck and jaw screaming. 'The story that you wanted. Almost better than a Nazi cabinet, don't you think?'

Patrick waved Julian out the front door and turned back to me on the landing.

'Unlike other men of my means, I take no satisfaction in winning.'

He looked genuinely sorrowful.

'Thank you for the company – and the story. I'll have Julian send you an invitation to the next gathering, should you change your mind, and the money will be in your account by the morning.'

He pointed a crooked finger at the couch.

'It's got nothing to do with him, but somehow it has everything to do with him. I understand.'

Patrick moved gingerly towards me and opened his arms for a hug. It lasted a very long time. While I inhaled his aftershave, I thought about Enzo and who he might be holding at that moment. I imagined it was him embracing me in our beautiful flat, between all our stuff, Lola prancing by our feet. And then in my mind's eye, the furniture all melted away and the breakfast bar instead became that sticky bar in Dalston, and it was loud and frenetic and the sweaty room whirled, and it was sardined with people and kick drums and synths and the band was great but it was so hard to hear a fucking thing, until out of nowhere, Enzo appeared, hair ruffled, shirt open and stood up on his tiptoes and shouted, clear as day . . .

*'Is okay to buy you a beer?'*

*

The money arrived just after midnight, along with a Marketplace message from Patrick. Attached as files were a copy of Julian's appraisal and an additional authenticity report from the auctioneer, confirming the value of Christie's old purple couch at between £15,000 and £20,000. Patrick had opted for the higher figure.

> Patrick. 00.54
> let me know if u need some advice on how
> 2 spend it 😉

# INTERMEZZI: DUST

Elly wakes up with dust in her eyes. It starts around seven or eight months after he leaves, this daily sensation of grit, interference. At first, she chalks it up to the general static that tends to accompany any hangover, a state she has been living beneath more or less constantly since cancelling their joint bank account and changing their Netflix password. Elly pays no mind to the irritation in her vision as it mostly spars with what's going on between her ears. She slips on the thick black Gentle Monster sunglasses that she has taken to using as a protective force field – even when it's overcast, especially if it's raining – and heads out the door to face the day regardless. But the mystery dust persists. It hangs around well beyond her spree of self-immolation. Elly wakes annoyed before she's even greeted the morning, feeling it cling to her eyelashes, making a bed below her eyelids in small dust depositories she can feel but never see.

It is the type of affliction her local GP, backed up for hours with old Hackney fixtures actually *dying* of something, would probably laugh her out of his office for, so Elly instead consults the ancient sages of Google and Reddit, who collectively suggest antihistamines that make her drowsy, or angry, depending on the type, eyedrops that burn like peeing with a UTI, saging her flat, which sets off her fire alarm and sends Lola screeching out the tall window by the couch, taking charcoal, which serves only to seal her sphincter shut for twelve days, and seeing a tarot reader, around which time her phone pings, politely informing her that she is clean out of data and any more forum-trawling while on the Overground is likely to cost her dearly.

Throughout her voyage across the lands of alternative medicine, the dust continues. Jess from her office, who has been wearing big bifocals since before they swung back around to become geek-chic, notices Elly's frustration.

'I also get that when my contacts don't line up properly,' she sympathises. 'It's the worst.'

Touched by the real interest of another human, Elly nods, scrunching her eyes shut and willing the specks to vanish. She does not have the wherewithal to tell Jess that she has in fact had 20/20 vision her entire life.

As the dust continues into its fifth straight week, Elly decides to get scientific. In an effort to capture the elusive substance and study it, she places plastic containers on Enzo's vacant side of the bed. She drapes a thin white muslin from the bedhead to the foot like she's some sort of frontierswoman setting up camp in an African desert and trying to evade mosquitoes, hoping she'll find traces of it in the morning. Elly moves to the backup couch she's borrowed from Oli for two days, passes out in the loft where there's no longer any furniture. She even resorts to going home with another designer she knows has fancied her for ages, only to collapse with exhaustion before anything can transpire. But the dust seems to defy any and all rules of logic. It stalks her invisibly, striking only when she's achieved a sustained level of deep sleep that renders her powerless to fight it off. Never in her ears, up her nose or silently coating her tonsils, the highly targeted specks ensure she arrives each day at work looking like she's been crying when she hasn't or like she's coming off a bender that has yet to begin.

In fact, Elly has not cried very often since her life was drone-bombed into the ash that she now futilely attempts to blink away as she crawls down Commercial Street in search of coffee. Certainly not spontaneously, as one would expect from someone whose wedding ring is still fresh enough that it barely leaves a tan line when they leave it in the bathroom, but who still slips it back on most days, just to remind themselves they were once another person's entire life plan. Elly has been most upset when she's had to flog stuff: the silver bike to Will, the record to Xenia. It takes seeing something physically walk out the door to get her going and every time she watches one of their possessions leave in the hands of another person, she sees, in split screen, Enzo arriving home with it the first time.

Elly watches as her boyfriend, fiancé, husband, ex-husband does things for her that she is sure no one else ever will. She sees him wheel Roxy quietly through the double doors, pausing to retie the shiny ribbon around her gleaming silver frame. She watches as he picks up the record from the framers, holding it close to him on the 58 bus, zipped beneath his puffer like it's contraband. She follows as he scours the aisles of HMVs up and down the city in their final glory years to find a box set of *The Sopranos*, dragging it home with him on the Central line, breaking a sweat at the effort. This cinematic sadness has only happened a few times and it is these moments for which Elly banks up her anguish. It is a move that is deliberate. It's not that she doesn't want to go into emotional overload whenever she hears Jessie Ware, Klaxons or even that ridiculous JME song he used to put on at full blast while he made coffee in the morning. Elly is just in the business of keeping her shit together. It's clear that Enzo isn't coming back; he hasn't so much as popped by to pick up his mail, let alone the rest of the items in his closet. He appears to be screening her calls. If it's true that her husband has vanished, potentially to another floor of the same building or all the way back to the Neapolitan coast, then it is also true that Elly is in some ways responsible for that, and to collapse into a bowl of salty, grief-stricken custard that she imagines would be her fate is not in any way helpful.

Besides, Elly is not sad. She is fucking agitated. She is over not being able to see, this constant feeling like she's being assaulted, plagued by forces as microscopic as atoms. Elly has recently taken to pulling down her bottom eyelids on the Overground, using her make-up mirror to inspect her eye sockets for clues. Even by East London standards, this is something else, and by Cambridge Heath, she typically has space, if not an entire quadrant of seats, to herself. She becomes one of those people you see sometimes in Shoreditch who stop and swear at nothing in particular, rubbing her face until it flushes, scratching the rims of her eyes until they are rusted and raw.

After six weeks, she sits down at her desk and finds a box of contact lenses with a Post-it from Jess, who has just gone on holiday. 'Try these,' it reads, surrounded by smiley faces. 'You deserve some relief.'

Closing her eyes becomes one of the few ways Elly can soothe them, so she starts going to bed far earlier than she needs to. She gainfully attempts to cut back on the rampant coffee addiction she's picked up from Enzo, but it doesn't last. Instead, she drinks about ten cups of tea between lunch and close and peaks too early, spending 7–9 hours a night fully wired, staring at the tiny granules drawing psychedelic shapes behind her eyelids. It's around this time that she finally accepts a dinner offer from Himesh, whose daughters are too kind to mention her brittle, blurry red eyes.

Elly's bloodshot season (which she doesn't yet know will soon be coming to an end) with its fragmented, obscured vision, the sheer bloody exhaustion of it all, is a physiological distraction. An inelegant one, to be sure, but it nonetheless achieves its aim of zeroing Elly's attention in on the tangible minutiae of her existence, conveniently diverting her itchy gaze away from the far more pressing and significantly more insurmountable issue: that she is a few days off turning thirty-seven and is devastatingly lonely for the first time since her parents' marriage fell apart.

As she rubs her eyes with the back of her palms for the fifteenth time one Wednesday morning, a new Slack message pops into the corner of her screen. It's from her boss; not Jack, her creative director, but Nick, one of the two managing partners. In the many years she has worked at Gilbert + Short, Elly has had precisely two conversations with Nick – one when he hired her and the other when she played her own music over the office speakers by accident and blasted Wolf Alice so loud she probably could have broken a window. She'd had her noise-cancelling headphones on and had kept jacking the volume, thinking they were on the fritz, without realising she was controlling the sound across the entire two floors of the business. He'd been a good sport about it, especially given the most monied and conservative clients had been in the boardroom at the time, clutching their ears in agony. But that was also ages ago.

It occurs to Elly that she is probably about to be fired. The dust situation isn't exactly public knowledge and Nick must think she's showing up to work stoned every day. *Christ*, she frets, fumbling around her handbag for the piss drops from hell, which she squeezes into the corners of her eyes, grimacing. *Just my luck.*

Nick's office, which is actually just a desk that faces out the window partitioned by two semi-circular arrangements of fiddle-leaf figs, is positioned away from the rest of the open-plan set-up. Unlike Max, the other partner, who likes to sit in the thick of it, like a general enmeshed within his battalion, Nick practises a casual aloofness which makes him far more respected, but also inordinately feared. Elly arrives at the wall of expensive baby trees. Through their fat, flat leaves, she can see Nick standing by the window, wielding what looks like a chunky Sharpie. He is drawing plans directly onto the glass, like some naughty four-year-old armed with a whiteboard marker. There is nothing that could conceivably pass for a door, so Elly rustles the leaves, hoping they'll announce her arrival. Finishing whatever it is he's sketching, Nick waves his hand behind his back, beckoning for her to come in. She gingerly sits in the only chair, hoping it isn't his.

'How are you then, Elly?' he asks, capping his pen.

'I'm . . . I'm fine thanks, Nick.'

'Really? Because I'm sure I'm not the first to deliver this brilliant insight and I mean this with the utmost concern, but you're looking a tad . . . is splotchy the right word?'

Elly, who is still trying to mentally compute if this is the sort of meeting where she is allowed to laugh, does so awkwardly. 'You could say that, yes.'

She sounds like what happens if you try to get an AI program to tell a joke.

'Is everything alright? This has been going on for some time, from what I gather.'

'No, all good, really,' she says brusquely, trying to change the subject. 'I'm just having this problem with my eyes. I think it's dust in my flat, maybe? Anyway, it's genuinely doing my head in.'

Nick frowns.

'Dust. When was the last time you had it cleaned?'

'Oh, it's nothing like that. It's more like particles or something. They get into my eyes while I'm sleeping, like a sort of succubus. Irritates me all day, you know? I walk around looking like I'm bonkers, trying to rip out my corneas.'

'Lovely image, truly,' Nick says. 'I trust you've tried all the remedies, but it doesn't sound like hay fever or something allergy-related.'

'I've replaced everything short of the bed frame,' she says, wearily. 'Changed laundry powder, stopped eating garlic, then chocolate, then apples. I'm starting to think, quite honestly, that I just have an aversion to my own existence.'

Deep in Nick's subconscious, an HR alarm bell dings. He rearranges his face to make it look more like that of a concerned father.

'You're not . . .'

'Oh god. No. No no no. Please, don't worry.'

'Okay, good. Great. You know, we don't get to talk much, but you're very important to us here.'

Elly stops pulling at her cuticles, a tactic she's recently employed to keep her hands away from her face.

'Wait, so I'm not getting the sack?'

Nick holds her gaze for a long time, before collapsing into a mess of amused sniggers.

'Sack you? What on Earth for?'

'The eyes, I don't know,' she offers meekly. 'Looking unprofessional?'

'Listen, what you do with your face is up to you. As for appearing unprofessional, Rob has worn both shorts and

Birkenstocks to client pitches this past summer, so I think you'll have some stiff competition on that front.'

Elly smiles widely. It's an expression that has fallen into such chronic disuse in the past year that it feels like her cheeks might shatter.

'I'll be honest with you,' he continues, 'we're a small shop. Word travels. So yeah, we heard what happened with your fella. Bloody awful thing, especially after all that time. And I just called you in here to tell you that even though he was a fun little bugger, what matters to us is you. That's not just me, either; it's Max, James, the whole team . . . even beach boy Rob with his German sandals. Frankly, we knew something was up when you started spending a lot more time in here after hours. Never took you for a late-night person and Max and I could tell that you were avoiding something at home. Now, I know what that feels like; truly I do. But if you just keep it all locked in there, well, there's nothing we can do about it. You've been here for an age, Christ, you're practically family. Talk to us. You need some time off, you need a new project, you need to drink wine with lunch, you need someone to high-five you each afternoon before you leave, just name it, alright? It's yours.'

He pauses to swallow, trying to bring some lubrication back to his throat.

'When I was about the same age you are now, I had my heart ripped out. Proper brutal, dumped on our five-year anniversary. Even thinking about it now, ten years on, it hurts like I've been stabbed. Nothing's as bad as that. Nothing. Look, I'm sorry for talking your ear off, but you just can't handle something of this magnitude alone. I know it from experience. So we're going to help you. All of us.'

Sensing that he may have already said too much, Nick stands up abruptly and goes over to the window, ostensibly to finish drawing whatever kitchen island he was in the middle of before Elly came in.

Elly blinks twice.

She wonders if she has finally done the unthinkable and fallen asleep at the office, that this entire exchange is part of some extended lucid dream sequence. But then she feels it. The silver pound dropping into the coin-operated binoculars shuttered behind her raw, red eyes. The fuzz being replaced by focus, at last. It's the precise moment Elly forgets about her eyes and remembers how much she misses companionship. The acknowledgement that she is lonely arrives alongside a flume of tears that blast away the flecks and specks and granules and filaments from their secret bunkers. And the realisation is not just that she is lonely, but that she is truly alone; marooned in her beautiful flat amid an ocean of regret. It's unfortunate that this understanding occurs in public, but perhaps it always needed to. It has been weeks since she's been able to see, but now what is vital to Elly in this moment, as water sluices through the jagged edges of her corneas, is that someone else does. Someone she knows intimately. Someone she trusts. Someone who isn't just passing through her life, buying items she once owned that represent a life she no longer has. By calling her in and calling her out, Nick has rendered as more than a sketch those few lines that exist simply to hold together negative space.

Much like her hurt, Elly is real. This is a terrible realisation, but in that moment, she has never felt more thankful for it.

She does not know how long she cries for, in the office of the boss who has offered her his friendship, but she does know that when it ends, the dust will have been banished, Elly will rejoin the ranks of the clear-eyed and the real work will begin.

# THE BEGINNING, WHERE IT ENDS.

Enzo always pulled out.

It was a tacit agreement he and Elly had honoured for almost the entirety of their relationship. It had taken them less than a year to dispense with condoms. Elly said it was like fucking a shrink-wrapped cucumber from Lidl, and Enzo, who was loath to encourage anything that might stand in the way of more sex, didn't disagree. It was autumn the first time they did it without protection, in Elly's Hoxton flat, Friendly Fires pumping through the Bluetooth speaker she nicked from Adriana's room to paper over the giggling and moaning. Elly was taken away in the moment; legs wrapped around Enzo, clinging to the shitty Argos headboard until the very last possible second, when she least wanted to slow down but nonetheless abruptly rolled off her boyfriend, leaving him to make a significant mess of her sheets.

Elly had started birth control when she was fourteen, forced into a corner by the unannounced twin arrivals of puberty and intense acne, but had done away with it before she'd even lost her virginity. The miracle pill of feminism that her grandmothers had marched for and the NHS would cover for decades had not agreed with her temperament, which was a polite way of saying it sent her completely fucking bonkers. With her mother all but disappeared by this point, it was up to Gary to somehow manage a daughter whose mood swings had surpassed standard teenage fare and quickly entered the realm of terrifying. Elly had never rowed with her pa, but now it seemed she couldn't stop; slamming doors hard enough to break them off their hinges, refusing to leave her room to eat dinner, bawling him out at the slightest provocation. Worried sick, Gary broke his own rules and reached out to his ex-wife, who matter-of-factly chalked it all up to adolescence, laughed at his prudishness and hung up the phone mid-conversation. Deferring then to science, the only authority he knew to be reliable, Gary eventually deduced his daughter was reacting to the excess oestrogen and progesterone in her once-daily tablet, and in a rare moment of calm, suggested she wean herself off it. Elly didn't have to be asked twice. She flushed the rest of her pack and never looked back, emerging from her hormonal haze with a brighter disposition and little inclination to ever try any alternatives.

By her mid-twenties, Elly was a firm proponent of the idea that effective contraception was a joint responsibility. Despite this, she walked into her relationship with Enzo having narrowly avoided a number of close calls with Ian, Brad and some other forgettable boys masquerading as men. Much like the pill that haunted her teenage years, the morning-after edition had a tendency to wreak havoc on her body, so for the most part, she played it safe. Besides, if she and Enzo were going to roll the dice, there were ways to play the odds in her favour.

'I'm sorry about that,' she said sheepishly.

'Is fine.'

'No, I should have warned you.'

Elly, trying to rectify the sheet situation, had realised it was most likely impossible, and instead began hastily stripping the duvet as they talked in the hushed tones that always tended to directly follow sex.

'I'm . . . not on the pill.'

'Birth pill? Is free, no?'

She sighed.

'It's free, but it's also bloody poison.'

'Che cosa?'

'It affects me. Mentally.'

'Si, okay. My cousin Chiara, same. Cry all the time.'

'Exactly. I'm not going through that again.'

She sat on the edge of her bed. Enzo moved over to her and began scratching her back. 'What about other things?' he murmured.

'Oh, you mean like shove a metal slinky up my vagina? Or a small parachute?'

Enzo thought on it for a minute.

'So, we go back to the condoms?'

'No, I think we just keep doing what we did tonight. Hasn't failed me yet.'

(It had, but having not yet effectively tracked her ovulation cycle, Elly was unaware of just how close she'd soared to the sun.)

'But maybe on me next time,' she said. 'I don't have that many spare sets of sheets.'

Implicit in any conversation around contraception is a parallel discussion about children. It wasn't something Enzo felt necessary to emphatically bring up early on in his courtship of Elly, but as the years rolled on and he entered his thirties, still climaxing onto his girlfriend's stomach or back, the distinct absence of any such chat was starting to grate at him. When they'd first begun dating, over dinner at Green Papaya, Elly's favourite Vietnamese spot in Hackney, he'd casually floated the idea. While he fiddled with chopsticks, implements he'd never quite been able to master, he asked Elly how many kids she'd like to have, hypothetically speaking. It seemed to him a relatively innocuous question; part of a standard three-weeks-dating repertoire that included 'If you could do anything with your life . . .', 'Tell me about your worst job' and 'What's the most embarrassing thing you've ever done while hammered?' It appeared that Elly saw things differently.

'Oh, I'm never having kids,' she said, returning to her beef phở.

'Si, not now, but when we are the age . . .'

Enzo stabbed at a soy-splattered mangetout, trying to salvage a line of questioning already in freefall. 'You get older and change mind.'

'I very much doubt that.'

'Is different. We are young now. One day not so young. You have your last party summer and then you want bambini. I see it happen with my sisters, cousins.'

'Don't bet on it,' Elly said, not raising her eyes from the bowl.

'Okay,' he said, raising his glass weakly. 'Challenge accepted.'

Ten years pass before Elly and Enzo arrive back at the sticky summer night of the failed 2018 World Cup semifinal, as the Three Lions crash out against Croatia in extra time and grown men sob in the streets. The walls of Hackney's pubs are lined with misery, lager and sweat. It has all the makings of a catastrophe for the national psyche. It also happens to be the exact evening, during a heat-of-the-moment bedroom pit stop while dinner simmers, that Enzo doesn't pull out in time.

It's not clear at first whether he forgets, stops trying or does it deliberately. To Elly, it's irrelevant. She bolts to the bathroom, screaming bloody murder, which intensifies with each passing minute. Historically, Elly and Enzo have not had a fight last more than fifteen minutes. Full-blown disputes are not something either believe in; Enzo already famed for his ability to de-escalate and Elly not keen to repeat the shouting and shattering of crockery that coloured much of her childhood. This, then, will prove to be the exception.

'Oh shit, shit, *shit*!'

Elly storms out of the loo and starts flinging things around the bedroom, trying to find her knickers and jeans. Still very much naked, Enzo sits up, trying to figure out a way to defuse what he thinks could quickly become a real crisis.

'I'm sorry, I get carried away,' he says softly.

'You need to get me the morning-after pill,' she snaps. 'Now.'

'Okay, I go tomorrow, in morning.'

'No, *now*. Leg it.'

Elly's face and neck are a deep crimson. It's a shade that means business.

'What? Why so urgent?'

'Christ. Why do you think, Enzo?'

'Tell me.'

'You're ridiculous. What if I get pregnant?'

'Babe, you won't get pregnant; I pick it up tomorrow.'

'No, Enzo. Now . . .'

'It won't –'

'You're having a laugh, right? I track my ovulation. We're bang in the middle of the danger zone right now. Tell me you understand what I'm saying.'

'Okay, okay. Can we just relax for maybe ten seconds?'

'I can't have a baby right now, I swear down . . .'

'Hold on. Clarify per piacere: can't have one *now*, or *ever*?'

This is the moment that will burn itself into Enzo's brain, where the mood shifts and the rubber band pressing him and

Elly together begins stretching. What he'll forget in years to come is that he was the one to start pulling it.

'Oh my *god*!' Elly shouts. 'This isn't the time for your games, Enzo. Can we please just deal with this? If I am pregnant, we're running down the clock very fucking fast.'

He shrugs.

'So, what "if"? Is so bad? Is not like we don't want to start our own famiglia. Maybe fate make decision for us.'

'Is that what you call your lack of self-control? Or was this whole disaster just in your stupid master plan all along . . .'

'Elly, you are being very paranoid, really. Was mistake only.'

'This is just so classic *you*,' she groans. 'It's not like someone putting extra parmesan on your pasta, you know. This could be the rest of our lives.'

'If you are pregnant.'

'Yes, if I'm pregnant, which becomes increasingly fucking likely the longer we sit here and have a philosophical discussion about it.'

'But *if* you pregnant, this is good?'

Exasperated, Elly flops face-first onto the bed.

'No, Darling, it isn't.'

'I thought . . . is what we want.'

'Is this about going to get the pill? Fuck it. I'll go by myself. I don't care.'

'You do not listen to me.'

'Oh, I'm listening, Enzo. Let me check if I've got it right. You had your big stud finish and now you want to justify it as what – an act of heroism? Like I'm supposed to be thankful that your hyperactive swimmers are making a beeline for my eggs at peak fertilisation time.'

'I said already Babe, was accident.'

'It doesn't bloody matter! What matters is nuking what comes next, alright?'

Enzo is suddenly forlorn at the prospect of his sperm being bombed out of existence.

'Why would we do this?'

'I don't know, maybe because someone just did the only thing you don't do WHEN YOU AREN'T WEARING A CONDOM.'

Elly rolls over so that she is lying directly next to Enzo. She focuses on the ceiling instead of him, hoping it will help calm the waves of rage rippling out from under her skin. There is a crack up there that she swears wasn't there before.

'Of course I know the rule,' he says. 'But is not, how do you say . . . relevant.'

'Enzo,' she replies, voice cold as a robot, 'the person who gets to decide if it's relevant is the person it's most relevant to.'

'You misunderstand. You not let me finish.'

'I already let you finish once. Look where that's landed us.'

Now it's Enzo's turn to lose patience.

'Is not relevant because this not a problem! Before, yes. But now –'

'Darling, don't be thick. Do you seriously want to have a *baby* right now?'

Elly's opened this door before. It's just a crack, barely a sliver, but it's more than enough for Enzo, who has just decided at this very moment that tonight is the night he wants to barge through it.

'Si,' he says, looking her dead in the eye. 'I do.'

'Well, I bloody well don't and last I checked, it was my body, not yours.'

'Explain to me, please. You always tell me to wait. I wait and wait. I wait years, Elly.'

'Don't do that.'

'Do what?'

'We talked about this. We said that next year we'd think about trying.'

Enzo laughs mirthlessly, which only serves to further infuriate his wife.

'What is your fucking problem? Did you just wake up this morning and think "Oh, yep, today's the day I go and get Elly pregnant." That should be a right bloody laugh for all your mates down at Bar Termini.'

Enzo still hasn't moved. Elly, meanwhile, is a hurricane, throwing clothes on and off the floor, not really looking for anything besides an excuse to keep being angry. She stops and glowers at him.

'Why aren't you getting your kit on?'

Enzo says the words slowly, like he's chewing on them. He wants to make it abundantly clear he isn't at all enjoying their taste.

'Next. Year.'

Elly explodes with impatience.

'Have you had a brain injury? Is this *funny* to you?'

'You say "next year" for five years, Babe,' he says, finally.

'No I haven't.'

'Si, don't make me idiot.'

He reaches for his phone, which is plugged in by the bedside table, opens it and starts scrolling.

'I remember the first time you say it. I remember because I text Sofia about it. I am excited to be a papa. And I make note, so I don't forget.'

He throws his phone across the ruffled sheets. There is a note highlighted on the screen. It is date-stamped: July 2013.

Emboldened by this evidence, he presses on.

'I come inside you, is accident. Honest – accident. Cara mia, who cares? We are married. We love each other. Isn't this time to try for un bambino?'

'Here's what I want to know . . .'

'. . . do you even want them? Bambini? Do you ever?'

'That's not what this is about.'

'*SI!*' he shouts, surprised at his own volume. 'Cazzo! Is precisely what is about. Elly, you thirty-six years old.'

'Oh, so it's about my bloody *age* now . . .'

Enzo's mood turns volcanic right as the smoke detector goes off. Elly has left her famous beef curry simmering too long on the hob, fully intending on getting back to it after their brief bedroom digression and not having anticipated the entire evening going south quite so swiftly. Clearly miffed at having been neglected, the expensive pan has now started belching plumes of spicy smoke across the kitchen. Elly rushes out to the stove as Enzo quickly wriggles into some pants, trying to remember which broom is tall enough to hit the alarm's kill switch. In the meantime, he remains very much invested in the first argument in many months he might actually win, though at what cost, he's not yet sure.

'Is about age, yes. Older you get, harder to be pregnant. You know this.'

Elly splutters as she pulls the Le Creuset off the heat and heads over to open the arched windows to try and let the smoke out.

'I . . . I can't have a child now. It would be mad.'

'Questa è una stronzata! We make money, good money. You get maternity from your job. People do it with less.'

'Why is this your decision?' she yells, trying not to burn her hand on the handle, which has turned radioactive. 'What happened to us being a team?'

'*Team!?*' he spits. There is venom in his throat. 'Is all about you! I ask you, before we get married, I say I no want anything except kids. You remember? Or I make this up too? Inventato!'

The smoke seems to be getting worse; Enzo and Elly can barely see two feet in front of them, which strangely makes it easier to tear strips off one another.

'No,' Elly hacks and coughs. 'I remember.'

'And you say what?'

'I said yes, I'd love to have children with you. When the time is right.'

Enzo strides through the fog of singed garam masala.

'So tell me this, and then we go get your pill. Can't have one now, or . . .'

Suddenly, mercifully, the shrieking from above cuts out. The entire flat stinks like a bazaar that's just been firebombed. Elly is bent over the sink, blubbering, and Enzo doesn't even need to finish the question. He tears back into their bedroom and begins manically packing his big overnight tote bag as his world collapses around him. Ten years, his entire youth, up in smoke. It should be poetic, but Enzo hates poetry. His entire brain screams with swear words in his local dialect, which knock about his skull as a means of distracting him from engaging with the gravity of the situation. He should return to the kitchen and check on his wife, but as we already know, he doesn't.

Errant fumes from the smouldering pan have escaped into the main hall, tripping off the building's system, alerting the fire station nearby. It's still hazy as hell in the flat as Enzo jimmies open the stiff bedroom window, sliding his bag and then himself out sideways. He doesn't remember to close it, a fact taken advantage of by Lola, the first responder, who makes it inside before the firemen do. She finds Elly exactly where Enzo left her; hands gripping the granite, tap running over the wreckage of dinner, steam rising with the Academy's alarm now howling on an endless loop.

And when help finally arrives, she mistakes the banging at the door for Enzo, who has forgiven her, come back for her and will wait many more interminable summers because he loves her in spite of the ways she does not love herself, and she flings open the door to a bemused gaggle of firemen, smoke billowing out behind her like a Disney animation, and yells clearly at the top of her lungs the same thing she told him right at the very beginning, which she now sees, finally, was already the end:

'Never! Never never *never*!'

# VII. LUGGAGE

If you could put a decibel meter next to commuters on a Friday afternoon Virgin Pendolino out of Euston, the sound Elly makes when the conductor announces the next station is Stockport would probably fry its internal mechanism. Elly loathes Manchester for what it represents – abject personal failure. A return to her father's Parsonage Road home for reasons that don't include Christmas, the wedding of a school friend or a dangerously maxed-out Monzo is practically unfathomable to Elly, who has spent nearly fifteen years pretending she is from somewhere else, a place where the people are cooler, more worldly, and less intolerably friendly. Elly slams back the last of the second canned G&T she'd bought in the restaurant car back at Milton Keynes, where they'd found out someone had jumped in front of the train, a development which had been announced like it was nothing. 'A person on the track,' the crackling voice had relayed over the speaker while they sat there suddenly motionless, as if it were just the usual spot of bother, some kindly old man who had gotten lost on his evening constitutional, not a forty-year-old now more closely resembling a Jackson Pollock and a driver traumatised for life.

A few hours before leaving for Euston, Elly knocks on Oli's door, Lola bristling in her arms. In her many years inhabiting Academy Apartments, she has still not figured out who the cat belongs to, and her sympathetic neighbour is as close as she'll get. Oli's flat is noticeably bigger than hers; he lives with two other housemates, though she's never actually seen them. He told her once that they both work in film and spend weeks at a time away on shoots, but she has decided that he's quietly loaded and living in the huge space alone, a bit like her.

'She keeps sneaking in here,' she says when he answers, still wearing pyjamas at two in the afternoon. 'I have this paranoid fear that I'm going to lock her in there for a week while I go away and she'll starve to death.'

'Unlikely,' Oli laughs, wrangling Lola into his flat and closing the door behind him. 'She's got at least ten other flats here on the go. Milk and tuna on demand.'

'Still, can you look after her for me? Sometimes I feel like she's all I have left.'

Elly refuses to get emotional about an animal that isn't even hers, but somehow it seems to be happening anyway.

''Course. Enzo still not back, then?'

'I believe that ship has well and truly sailed.'

'Ah. Balls. Sorry to hear that. If it helps though, Mum called me the other day and told me to get a "proper" girlfriend and settle down, so I guess you can just let me know when you're ready.'

'Oli, I know you're by yourself in there. You know how long it will take them to find your body after I strangle you?'

'You know, I'm quite into that,' he jokes.

'Practically buzzin' at the thought of it. In the meantime, Lola drinks full-fat milk. Semi-skimmed makes her a bit loopy.'

Oli nods sagely, like he hasn't also been feeding Lola her second or third supper for the better part of his twenties.

'Off to see your dad up in Manny, then?'

'Don't be silly,' she lies unconvincingly. 'I'm going to Ibiza.'

The notoriously bendy train careens on its tracks, a two-hour-long flat rollercoaster ride made worse by the fact that Elly has drawn the short straw and is sitting backwards. She rubs her tired eyes and tries to allay the queasiness by imagining she's heard the man wrong, and she is pulling into Stockholm instead, where everybody dresses like her, and she is miraculously of average height. Elly is distracted from her parallel universe by an accent from the seat behind her that has to be 85 per cent nasal. It is the voice of her people, of Liam and Noel, of Vera and Jack Duckworth, singsong sentences and flat vowels, thick like paint that never truly dries. She hears the phrase 'dead nice' and an involuntary shudder runs through her body. There's no escaping it; Elly will always be a Manc.

She hasn't given her pa the full rundown, and it's unlikely Christie will be around, having shacked up with the local dentist her pa always hated and chosen to spend most of the winter chasing rays on package tours that take in everyone's favourite fading jewels of the Commonwealth. Elly has a sixth sense for when her mother's river of unsolicited holiday photos with her latest beau will start flowing in from Barbados, or Morocco, or Sri Lanka. It's something she's more attuned to than the cycles of her own period. She never replies to any of them. That she's returned to Stockport at its most grim – during a limp, damp spring that feels more like the winter that preceded it – is partly out of necessity, but mostly opportunistic; if she's going to leach the sorrow out from the many protective layers enveloping her soul, it would be better to do it in the presence of the parent she can still have supper with without turning into Bruce Banner.

So it's Gary waiting for her on the station platform at 11 pm, even though she told him three times she could take a taxi, arms by his side to stop himself from hugging her immediately, something he knows she instinctively recoils from. Gary's EQ is so high he could run whatever the Mensa equivalent is for the world's most sensitively powerful men. He is so good at listening, parsing and understanding people it remains a mystery to Elly why her mother would have ever considered leaving him to hook up with another man. Even in his mid-seventies, Gary has hung on to his looks, key features of which, like his searing hazel eyes, dead straight hair and affable, rosy complexion, he has transferred to his daughter.

This time it is Elly who seems to have abandoned her trademark self-control. She launches in as soon as she sees Gary, leaving her borrowed bags spinning on the platform. She finds herself pulled towards her father without even realising it and they grip each other for a long time, Gary somewhat stunned at this change of pace but, realising this might be the last time he experiences an embrace so genuine, holding on as tightly as possible. The train departs, the few remaining passengers eventually locate an Uber and it is only when it is eerily, pristinely quiet that Elly and her pa finally peel apart.

'I have to say, this is not the service I've come to expect from Manchester Mini Cabs.'

'Well, times are tough in the transport game,' Gary says, always rising gleefully to the bait. 'We had to add a touch of class to our already sterling service, you know. Stay a few steps ahead of them new kids on the block.'

Elly takes a few steps back to retrieve her wheelie bag, which has inelegantly faceplanted over onto the concrete, arm fully extended.

'Sorry, I didn't quite get your name when I made the booking. It's Mohammed, right?'

'Jamal, actually, but that's fine. You Londoners are always a little bit racist.'

'That's very true,' Elly laughed. 'It's always a bit nicer up North.'

'Now, madam,' Gary continued, not missing a beat, 'forgive me for asking, but what on Earth happened to your real luggage?'

'Well Jamal,' Elly said, linking her arm through his as they headed for the parking lot. 'That's sort of why I'm here.'

**Sofia Mazzarella 07.55**
**Hi, is this still available?**

In my defence, would you remember the new surname of your ex-husband's freshly married sister? Enzo's insanely sprawling family was tricky enough to stay on top of, and that's before I got to his three separate uncle Gios, his nonna with the same name as her granddaughter and those dozens of cousins in between. The whole process of wiping out my past life on Marketplace had clearly taken a toll on my critical faculties, because there is no way on God's Earth I would have otherwise actively invited *this* Sofia into my house.

She stood expectantly with her hands on her hips, taking in the completely bare space. From her perspective, it probably looked like someone was squatting – or was about to start shipping out. I'd put the luggage by the breakfast bar, which remained the only thing left apart from the fridge. With Patrick's funds, I'd finally paid off my rent and had started actively looking into furniture, including lights that had once been way out of my price range. I was going to buy a proper record player. Finally, after nearly a year, my life was ready to start moving again. And now this.

'He doesn't know I'm here.'

'Okay.'

It didn't help that Sofia had always been Enzo's closest sibling and looked the most like him. Strikingly so, in fact. It was as if he'd returned to the flat in female form, which made the encounter distinctly more unnerving than it already was.

'He need luggage. To go back. And I say "No Enzo, is expensive. I find for you on Marketplace."'

'But you knew it was me.'

'You must understand, he has nothing. He left everything here. And now I see you sell it? You sell these things that are his?'

'They were ours, Sofia.'

She did exaggerated air quotes.

'"*Ours.*"'

It was a word that sounded strange in an accent.

'Well, you owe him half, no?' she challenged.

'Not really. They were sitting here waiting for him to come back and take. His clothes, his toiletries, his stupid grime memorabilia, all of it. It's all here.'

'But no couch. No chairs. No table. Table you bought in Firenze. Together.'

'Sofia, to be fair, I don't really owe you an explanation.'

'Sei una stronza! Che puttana!' she spat. 'Yes, you do.'

I'd seen Sofia arc up a few times before. I pulled back.

'Listen, try and see it from my side. He walked right out that door and never came back. Didn't call. Didn't text. Not a word. Nine months. What am I supposed to do, sit here and mope forever?'

Everything was eroding. All that work I'd done, the hours I'd spent stuffing Enzo into that bulging box called The Past, getting myself back onto an even keel. I was unspooling – spinning around while standing still. I held the breakfast bar for balance, trying to maintain the upper hand. I really thought I might be sick.

'You no call *him*! He's so sad. Patetico. He stay on my couch for weeks.'

'Sofia,' I said quietly. 'He left me.'

'So you make money off his things?'

'I'm not following. Has he lost his job? Does he need money?'

Sofia kicked the smaller suitcase in frustration, sending it spiralling off into the kitchen and banging into cabinets.

'You know why he left, Elly.'

I went to go rescue the case, which had now tipped over onto its side.

'Where we come from, lies like this hard to forgive.'

'Lies?'

'Si, lies. What else could it be? Enzo is thirty-five now. He is not young man.'

'Christ, thirty-five is not old! I'm nearly thirty-seven. We're not even middle-aged.'

This was not a conversation I wanted to have in the slightest. If someone in a balaclava were to corner me out on Chicken Shop Run, stick a knife up against my ribs and tell me I absolutely had to, I'd have chosen bleeding out in the laneway over chatting it out with Sofia. Enzo had often told me she looked up to me more than her own sister. It was one thing to disagree with your partner. Now I had the unique displeasure of letting down an entire family.

'You rob him of chance, chance to be young father,' she said. 'To be father at all.'

This was unfair and I could tell she knew it. I took the opening.

'Don't be so fucking dramatic. Nobody is robbing anybody. I just don't want kids right at this particular moment in my life. Am I not allowed any agency over my own body?'

'You know how hard it was to have Mia? I was not even thirty.'

'Of course I do. Enzo knew how I felt about all that stuff. Have you ever thought that not everyone wants to go through what you did? It's not predestined, you know.'

Sofia pulled out her tattered wallet. 'I buy these cases from you, which Enzo *bought for you*, so he can get on plane and go as far away from you as possible.'

I snorted a bit too loudly, trying to suppress the giggles again. I sounded like a lunatic. Perhaps that was the idea.

'These are matt black. You can buy them in literally any colour and yet the ones I have are black. Who do you think bought them? Enzo hates black.'

'But you love it. You black everything, always. He do anything for you.'

When she'd shown up, I'd worried that it would be hard to fight with Sofia. For a start, she was my favourite member of Enzo's family outside of his mother – and the only one who lived in England. I saw her more than my own parents. To make matters worse, the Espositos had always been so good at arguing. Their dinner table conversations sounded like furious debates even when they weren't. But now I found myself charging up. After everything, I didn't deserve another ordeal.

'You're rewriting history. I wanted a black bike, he got me a silver one. He talked me into getting that huge fucking table.

He bought me that record and then he framed it so we could never use it. It's always been about him.'

Sofia didn't even pause to consider what I'd said.

'Dottore, he say that at our age we are geriatric. Geriatric. You know this?'

'Yeah, I've read a women's magazine before.'

'Every year it become more impossible.'

'I know.'

'You know this and you tell my brother every year to wait. For what? Maradona to come back to Napoli?'

'Listen, I love Enzo. More than I've ever loved anything or anyone.'

'No, you don't. Someone who loves someone no do this. You are cruel.'

'I genuinely thought I would change my mind.'

'What is wrong with him? He is perfect man. Women, they love him.'

'They definitely do.'

'Is it sex?'

Fuck me. I couldn't have written this if I tried.

'It's not the sex.'

'You know what I think? I think Paolo is right; you are crazy.'

'Cool. You know, I might be.'

Sofia was welling up, and to add insult to injury, she couldn't undo the zip on her wallet. She was tugging at it but it wouldn't give, obviously trapped on one of the new plastic notes she was clearly planning on throwing at me.

'You're right, Sofia,' I said as I watched her struggle, silently praying the zip would break and this protracted torture session would be over. 'The cases weren't for me. They were for us. We were planning our honeymoon and Enzo said, "We are going to travel the world together. We need proper luggage." We liked these because they had in-built chargers and Enzo was always worried about his phone dying after long plane journeys.'

Sofia sniffled. 'Enzo worry a lot.'

'Si,' I said, without realising. 'He does.'

'I think he be an amazing papa.'

'Absolutely. Of course he would. But I . . . I'm not mother material. It's not in me. I don't feel it like you do, like other women do. That obsession, the longing to start a family, to have a baby of my own. I've known it for a long time, but I loved Enzo so much I thought I could hold on until the right switch flicked on, you get me?'

I'd never said this out loud to anyone. I'd imagined that when I did, I would feel different, like I'd purged something vile from my system. But all that was left was a faint stinging, as if I'd rinsed my insides out with bleach. I'd finally come out with it, this unattractive, unlovable secret, but I was telling the wrong person. What a classically me thing to do.

'Is scary to be a mother,' Sofia said. 'Everyone feels this.'

'It's scary, but you still wanted to do it. You wanted to do it so badly you kept going, even after the miscarriages. That's so much dedication. I can't even imagine it.'

'But I have Mia,' Sofia said, wiping her eyes with the backs of her hands. 'It was difficult, yes, but she is mine. And you will have nothing. And Enzo, he will have nothing.'

I held my hand out and took Sofia's wallet, pulling at it gently to loosen the zip. The cash, which was all in ten- and twenty-pound notes, sprayed comically across the floor. I got down on my knees, eager to focus on something that wasn't Sofia, and counted it up. It was all there.

'Before, you asked why I never called Enzo after he left. That's the reason. He deserves another shot. A real one. There is someone out there, probably lots of women out there, who can give that to him. He's only going to get more handsome as he ages, and he isn't going to lose his hair. He could have a baby by the spring.'

Sofia wheeled the small case over to sit beside the larger one. She looked at me for the first time with what seemed like genuine sympathy. My little Italian sister briefly snapped back into focus and I realised with some sadness that this was almost definitely the last time I would see her.

'Enzo and I get back together, all that happens is we prolong the inevitable. I know what he wants. And I know that I can't give it to him. Why make him suffer?'

'But is not suffering. He loves you. My brother cry for you every day. I cannot tell you how much he loves you. He do anything for you.'

'But not this, right?'

'No,' she agreed. 'Not this.'

'And I don't want to suffer, either. I need to keep going with my life, but I can't do that when Enzo still speaks to me from every corner of this flat. And before you ask, it isn't about moving somewhere else, because then he just travels with me, with all this shit.'

I waved my hand across my barren living space for dramatic effect.

'He needs to be gone; our stuff needs to be gone. It's the only way I'll ever be happy again, maybe, one day.'

I stacked the cash neatly and handed it back to Sofia. 'Those suitcases are the last pieces left of the two of us. Please, keep the money. Give them to Enzo. Let him travel, live his life. Tell him to call me and come pick up his clothes. Tell him Lola is still here every night and she misses him. That I'm still wearing his ring, that I'll always wear it. And tell him that I'm sorry.'

I helped Sofia out the door with the cases. I heard her wheeling them down the bumpy alley towards the bus that would take her back to Clapton, where she would relay the events of this most unbelievable afternoon to Paolo and little Mia. I headed back inside and felt Lola skip between my feet as I closed the door. I exhaled deeply and put on some very loud music. My completed 'to sell' list was still on the fridge, every item now crossed out in thick black Sharpie. I took it down, tore the paper carefully into tiny strips like it was a bank statement I didn't want fished out of the trash, and threw it away.

I texted Gary, confirming I'd be on the train back home the next evening and that I'd still be staying the week. It triggered a flurry of concerned questions, all of which I ignored for the minute. There'd be more than enough time to talk about it all when I got there.

In the meantime, I ripped a fresh sheet out of my journal and started writing a new kind of list. It covered the page, front and back, and I'd never been more excited by the prospect of its existence.

When I got back from Manchester, for the first time in what felt like forever, I was going to properly stock that fridge.

# TANTI AUGURI

It is Elly's fortieth birthday and it is one of the better ones. Patrick has graciously lent out his Marylebone townhouse for the event and though the space felt far too empty just a short time ago, guests have since started trickling through the French doors. Ed is greeting everyone by the entrance, putting on a show of pretending that this opulent palace is theirs. He catches her eye just as Himesh and Sonja barrel in, already drunk in anticipation of a night out without their daughters, and she thinks that although she does not love him with the intensity that she has loved before, he might be enough.

The invitation boldly proclaimed the death of Elly's youth, and relatedly, her thirties. Ed helped design it to look dangerously like a funeral notice, the easiest way to ensure everyone wore all black. The two of them met at her office, where Elly is now a Senior Associate and Ed occasionally leads special projects, but mostly flirts with her outrageously over email. He is not Scandinavian, but he is lovely.

While waiting for the real festivities to begin, Elly allays her nervousness by taking out her phone and wheeling mindlessly through Instagram. While she has a more legitimate use for social media than most of her peers, using it to source new inspiration from designers around the world, she primarily uses the app to ruthlessly stalk the ghosts of her past life, whose performative posting from holidays in Crete and Lisbon tends to bore her senseless. Elly's account is entirely comprised of photos of modernist chairs. Once considered totally weird, in the 2020s, such dedication has been rebranded as 'niche'. She has around 7000 followers and not a clue where any of them came from.

Despite consciously uncoupling their marriage, Elly and Enzo were never callous enough to do the same online. Perhaps it is their shared knowledge that this is the last sinewy string that connects them, an unwillingness to completely close the door on such a formative decade of their lives, Enzo having indeed moved out of London and Elly onto an entirely new life. She deleted Enzo's phone number not long after he left; this is now her only way to contact him. Each year they send each other polite direct messages on their birthdays, which are only a week apart. Elly should receive her next 'tanti auguri' on Monday.

Her eyes slide down the screen again, past friends from school holding Aperol Spritzes by the canal, videos of her boss and his mates at the football. As she has thought on many occasions just like this one, this app is a complete waste of time. She is about to put her phone back in her bag and re-enter the moment when her thumb stops, about two milliseconds before her heart does.

Enzo's babies are adorable. Twin girls, both fully drenched in his features. His partner has seemingly contributed minimal DNA to their composition, at least currently. The pair of them stare out at her from the screen, already covered in their tousled Enzo hair and their strong Enzo brows, wrinkling their little Enzo noses. He is balancing one on each knee and looks as if he has died and gone to heaven. Elly double-taps to zoom in, then pinches back out again. Her charcoal-glittered eyes brim. She has never experienced so many emotions in a single sitting.

He never did come by for his stuff, and after a full year had passed, both of their thumbs hovering over the green button on the million redrafted texts they'd never send, she boxed them all up and dragged them to Traid on Kingsland High Street, where they could be stickered, racked and resold to help those less fortunate. Most of them were still in decent nick. On the way back to get the final lot of shirts, she stopped and realised she'd been cutting through Shacklewell Lane, just by the pub where they first met. She was relieved to discover that she felt nothing. Sadness, still, but not one that seemed oceanic.

Elly looks up and surveys the room, which has now packed out. It is a strange melange of well-wishers, as any London milestone birthday tends to be. People have flooded in and melted away from her life in this transient city in ways she would never have divined as a young woman. Elly still lives in Academy Apartments, with Lola and a new set of furniture. Her dining table is smaller, rounder, more chic. The Chesterfield has been replaced by two armchairs in lurid purple, beside which sits a record player and two bookshelf speakers. She sourced it all on Marketplace.

Earlier that year, the label behind Sampha and Jessie Ware's 'Valentine' reissued the song on 7-inch vinyl for the first time in a decade. Elly did not buy it. The keepsakes of her relationship with Enzo are no longer physical.

Elly glances back at the photo of her ex-husband and his new daughters. She breathes in slowly through her nose and can just about magic herself back to that baking summer in Naples, eating focaccia in the shade beneath a tree in front of his parents' house. Her mouth tingles with salt and rosemary, and as she dusts the crumbs off her dress, she glances up and sees Enzo gazing at her. It is a look that says 'there is nothing else worth focusing on here but you'. A look rooted firmly in the now, the liminal space where she has come to know young love ultimately exists.

The first thing Ed remarked upon after spending the night at Elly's was how tastefully appointed everything was, like it was always meant to be there. It will take her a while to tell him the whole story, which she's not entirely sure she has straight anymore. The sharp edges seem blunter now. Her new bike is called Merlin. He is midnight black, semi-electric and gets her to work in under ten minutes.

Now Ed and her father make a beeline for her, glasses in hand. The mischievous look on their faces suggests they are going to make a toast, something she'd ordinarily shy away from. Tonight, though, she's strangely at peace with being the centre of attention. Nobody made a proper speech at her wedding. It's been a long while since she's been feted in a public setting. Maybe it will be nice.

The cursor sits in the comment section below the photos, blinking expectantly. For once, without pause, Elly has the words. Her dictionary still remembers a time when she texted the love of her life in poorly formatted Italian.

'Bellissima!' she types, slipping it back in her bag before she can unsend it.

Ed's arm finds its place around her shoulders. Gary sways imperceptibly under the influence of one ale too many. There is the sound of a fork tinkling against glass and with almost theatrical precision, the room falls quiet.

# VOWS

Elly,

This moment could not be more special to me. I have been dreaming of it since the night we met and I am so glad – *emozionato* – it is finally here.

From separate people born in different countries, we now unite to become una famiglia . . . which means soon you'll start talking with your hands and maybe I grow a few inches in my sleep.

I promise to make you as happy as you make me, which is every moment of every day.

I promise to cook you ragù in the winter and vongole in the summer, that our bellies and glasses will always be full.

I promise you a life full of *Andiamo!* – that we should always encourage each other to keep moving forward, even when is hard.

I promise that when we are old, nonna and nonno, that we will still walk arm in arm through the park and talk about our future.

I promise to make a big home together and fill with all the beautiful things you love.

I promise I be there for you, no matter what happens.

I promise to stop trying to buy you things that are not black.

I promise our figli won't be my height.

After we were together a few years, you tell me one day that you think our love is like Gucci. I ask what you mean, and you say because it is always reinventing itself into something beautiful, even when times are not so good.

I think this is excellent metaphor, and it is part of why I love you.

I look forward to many more years of being molto Gucci with you.

*

Enzo,

I think vows are very archaic and decidedly anti-feminist, but something I've realised in the ten years we've spent together is that when I'm with you, even the fusty old stuff feels new and exciting.

I know you wanted a big wedding. It's mad, really; all of our friends have tied the knot in Tuscany and Puglia and I end up marrying a red-blooded Italian in Hackney. But I don't think our love requires a huge audience to be validated. I never did.

All that matters is that you and I, with our wildly diverse

backgrounds, shoe sizes and colour preferences, have found something rare and vital in each other. I know this without table settings, without a registry, without a giant cake neither of us will eat. With you, Darling, I have nothing to prove.

But given that we dressed up so nicely and you look so handsome in your green velvet suit, I'll try my very best:

I vow to build a life together that is richer and happier than the one I came from, one that is full of joy and dancing and hot summers in Naples.

I vow to see the world as you do, because it is never as beautiful as when wearing your rose-coloured glasses.

I vow to be there for you whenever you are in crisis, not just as your wife but as your best friend.

I vow to let you help me, especially when I am unable to help myself.

I vow to remember the key differences between Stormzy and Skepta, and to let you rap both while you're making me breakfast.

I vow to smother you in a love I did not know I had in me until I met you, but now flows from me like water.

I vow to ride our matching bikes through the park and get baked goods together every Saturday morning, no matter where we live.

And finally, I vow that even though my Italian will never be as good as your English,

*Sei tutta la mia vita.*

You are my whole life.

# ACKNOWLEDGEMENTS

THIS BOOK, AS with all my work, would not be possible without my brilliant wife, Keren. The kernel of the idea that would eventually become this novel belongs to her, and I am grateful to her for allowing me to build it out into my own world. Writers are frustrating people to live with, but Keren, you make it seem easy. Every day with you is a new love story. As Enzo says, I am mad for you, and I look forward to Rae one day reading this by the beach on summer holidays with us.

Grace, whose name I had to attribute to a swinging '60s character in the book because you are truly a rockstar agent of the highest order, thank you. Pivoting from memoir to romantic fiction is no easy task, especially for a man, but you saw the potential as you always do and helped me fight to find it the right home. You're the best and I adore you.

Cate, my newest and favourite lunching partner. I knew that you got this book immediately and I've so enjoyed working with you on this. Your empathy and intelligence has served me well and I can't wait to do it all again on the next one.

My Pan dream team, Rufus, Allie and Brianne, thanks for taking this book on with such enthusiasm and loving it as your own.

George, I am in constant awe of what cover designers do and you have proven no exception. You really nailed it.

I am blessed to have great friends that I can rely upon as early readers. In the case of *All the Beautiful Things You Love*, I am indebted to Jessica Aureli, Georgie Koch, Danielle Rajendram, Hannah Nolan, Nell Whitehead and Justin Wolfers for their detailed and honest feedback.

I love Italy like it is my second home, but the language has always eluded me. On this front, I owe Francesco Piazzoni and Carlo Mazzarella a huge debt of gratitude for helping make Enzo sound as believable as possible.

To my family, who were extraordinary through the onslaught of very difficult press around *Ray*, thank you for continuing to believe in me as a writer and not asking me when I am going to find a real job as much as you used to. Particular thanks to David, who read and gave critical early feedback and Oma, who as usual never stopped asking to read it, even before it was finished.

*All the Beautiful Things You Love* is a work of fiction, but it borrows some elements that are real. Academy Apartments very much still exists beside Hackney Downs station, as does the wonderful Bar Termini in Soho. 'Valentine' really was released as a limited heart-shaped vinyl. Victoria Park remains a brilliant park to ride a bike through with no hands.

Most importantly, the book asks questions about the expectations we place on ourselves and our partners when it comes to children. I have seen firsthand the result of what happens when these are left unanswered. Women who choose not to have children are as vital to society as any other person, but we currently only accept this response from men. Elly is inspired by many of the phenomenal women in my life who have decided that motherhood was not their path.